Hunter's Moon
THE PRECINCT

By

V J GARLAND

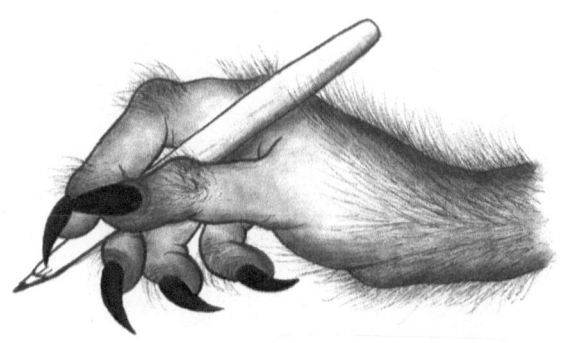

I0593605

V.J.Garland

The Precinct: Hunter's Moon Book #3 by V.J.Garland

Published by V.J.Garland

https://vanessajgarland.com/

For permissions contact: vgarland89@outlook.com

Book Cover Illustration by Angie Liu

Editor: Joey Prosser

ISBN: 978-0-6487069-8-4

ISBN: 979-8-3789506-9-0

First Edition.

Genre: Thriller/Fantasy/Horror/Romance

Summary: The Precinct was meant to be a haven, an escape for those in need, those cursed to a life they didn't choose for themselves, seeking refuge and some semblance of regular life. But anarchy begins to unfold in the village as newcomers try to discredit Jax and question the delicate balance of a human supply chain. Meanwhile, Seattle has been overrun with werewolves as a rare celestial event lingers over them. The past will return to haunt Jax, and his friends as they battle their demons from every angle. Life as they know it will change forever.

Printed in Australia.

V.J.GARLAND

Hunter's Moon

V.J.Garland

V.J.GARLAND

Hunter's Moon

Jax Retribution

V.J.Garland

Prologue:

LETTER'S

FOR

LUPINA

Dear Lupe,

I feel Kyle's presence in every moment of my day. I can hear his voice, telling me to press on and then I feel the cold rush and see the vision of life leaving his body. Every day I wake up, without any real lasting purpose. I know the sanctuary we've created will one day crumble, I can feel the tension already building, but what does it make me if I turn away those who wish to try? Should I have let Kyle kill me?

Here, I'm just barking orders, maintaining a fragile system. Inflaming an already tense situation every time I leave my cabin and I only do so to ensure control stays in my hands.

There have been so many come and go, most part on good terms. But some haven't, they've gone on to create their own societies, ones that cater to their own desires. Others linger a little longer...

It's a dangerous little world.

Jax

V.J.Garland

Lupe,

I saw Noah and Jax do this, and I hope it's okay for me too.

Our days in solitude have become months— and months have turned into years. The Precinct is now overly populated, to the point of it being dangerous.

Word spread of a haven for werewolves and their human families, the bunker is well over capacity and thirty more cabins have been built on top of the original ten.

The bunker now mostly houses humans, the wives, partners, and one teenager, Alexa. Not many of the wolves are granted access inside, only the original eleven, those who first occupied the land.

It feels more like a prison half the time, but Celinde, nor I would ever dare say that out loud.

Arthur and Otis oversee fixing and building the cabins, they have a team of new wolves that help— the newcomers remain in the field at all times. There's Clarence who has been a werewolf for so long he couldn't even remember his birthday, he's what I'd call shady and then there's Graham, nobody trusts Graham. He's weak-minded and always licks his lips whenever a human walks past him. Christian does his best to limit these crossovers, but it's hard to avoid entirely.

Jake, Jamal, and Tristan have become unlikely best friends, they live in a shared cabin, which is one of the few that ever needs repairs. Arthur has a corner in the bunker dedicated to plastic window materials after he got tired of cutting his fingers on shards of glass so often.

Alexa had tried to run away multiple times, but she never gets too far. Mindy is in a constant spin and Jax has ordered guards to be set up every half mile, he's worried she'll talk, again. She's threatened Arthur and Jax on multiple occasions as most teenage girls do when they're caged like animals. She's eighteen now and sick of living inside a bunker. The last time Alexa left Willmore accompanied was a month after we first arrived, Mindy and Izzy had taken her to Kamloops for a supply run and she bolted to the police station reporting Kyle's disappearance. This didn't go over well with Jax, he had the police silenced— finitely silenced.

Over time he's grown into his role, he knows he can't afford to be the gentle leader anymore, he must be harder on everyone. Especially with Clarence and Graham trying to infiltrate the Precinct with whispers of weakness and gossiping that Jax had better quarters than most. He lets it slide though because most of us think they are senile.

But the truth is, Jax sleeps chained to his bed most nights, he has the smallest cabin which is reinforced with steel walls hidden beneath a layer of marine plywood. This wasn't made common knowledge, but Jax's eyes never changed back. They've stayed red after what happened on Cannon Beach all those years ago, no matter how much he tries to live a vegetarian by werewolf standard lifestyle. Over those difficult few months after Kyle's passing, we accepted that the only people able to talk him down were Tristan, Ezra, and Christian. Celinde and I were at too much risk and Jax made an obvious effort to stay far away from us, we barely spoke anymore unless to conduct business, I felt like we were strangers all over again.

Most humans aren't allowed anywhere near the cabins, food is prepared and kept in the bunker and there are two collection times a day. That includes Ezra and Christian, I can't remember the last time I shared a bed with Ezra. After Kyle *died, we kept our distance from one another for months, but it was inevitable. The heart wants what the heart wants, and we had even discussed leaving together, I knew he was trustworthy, and he had more control than anyone else here, but then a flood of newcomers rained down upon us and Jax asked Ezra to stay, that was three years ago now.*

Celinde refused to leave Christian, and Christian didn't have the heart to leave Jax. So, we all just stayed and hoped the glory days would be around the next corner, but it just gets worse. Winter is always the hardest. Mindy stockpiles for months, but the snow gets too thick out here and we can't get the cars out down the dirt road— it's never enough.

Austin has taught Izzy and Mindy how to use the greenhouse and we have a decent flow of vegetables. Tristan just hunts a lot, he never got over that incessant hunger, but he seems to be able to stave it off better, away from humans. He leaves freshly dead animals at the bunker door weekly, and it became my job to butcher them. I have the strongest stomach, that's what Mindy says. It's a good excuse to open the doors and get some fresh air at least. Ezra comes up with Tristan and I steal what kisses and hugs I can in the short time we have together, he rarely ventures inside for long, and the relationship is starting to feel more like convenience or habit than anything.

Kitty was the only one who escaped, Jake made sure she got away, and she never came back after what she saw Jax do to Kyle. She took Jake's car and the last we saw of her was a dust trail. I wish so often I'd gone with her.

I think I know how you felt, Lupe. Writing to you is the only solace I have, you're the only one who understands how completely lonely this is—even when you're surrounded by others.

They are part of Jax's well-oiled machine now, a very numb machine. I wish I knew you; we'd have been friends!

Carrie.

CHAPTER ONE

CELINDE

Day of Kyle's Death

Carrie rested in the bloodied snow for hours—even after we had buried Kyle's body.

Her eyes were empty, and sorrow consumed all her being. I knew she blamed herself for Kyle's rage. I laid beside her and held her eyes in mine, but I couldn't promise it would get better, I couldn't even promise her tomorrow. So, I gently grasped her hand and pulled her into me and let her scream and weep every tear she had left—if any at all.

I don't know whose sorrow was more deafening—Carrie's or Jax's.

It was this night that I learned just how loud grief could be, you could see it, hear it, even smell it. For a moment in time, it consumed all things and shut out the rest of the world. It demanded all focus and left you empty with a pounding headache and a staleness to your body you wouldn't be able to shake for days to come.

Grief did that, it lingered until you peeled yourself from the foundation you laid upon, some of us just took longer than others to get up.

My poor Carrie, she embodied passion and excitement, and she felt loss at the same magnitude.

Ezra and Tristan sat a few feet away from us, enough so she wouldn't know they were there, but *they* needed to feel close to her. Tristan wept silently, he felt responsible for Kyle's outburst on top of the loss of his entire family. Ezra was keeping him close while Christian watched from the hill as Jax massacred an entire field of trees. It felt like thunder and lightning were crashing into the valley, the earth shook with every tree Jax slammed into the ground and snow pelted down each time he uprooted a log and stripped it of roots and branches.

"I'm sorry, Care," I sniffed as I brushed her dark curls off her face.

She couldn't reply between sobs, she just heaved and struggled to catch her breath.

"This wasn't your fault…" I assured her.

"He came here because of me, I should have known better," she cried.

"How could you have? After all these years, none of us knew," I tried to assure her.

She inhaled a deep breath and sat up wiping her eyes.

The silence was deafening as Jax sunk into the snow numb of emotions.

Days and weeks passed, but Jax never came back to the bunker, he stayed in the valley building until he had no resources left.

His human form was pale and lean. He was depleted and running on nothing, but the cold crisp air and it began to show. Every so often he'd disappear for several days at a time and come back with a little more color to him and his bulk returned, but he was quiet, his presence even more commanding than before.

Tristan would always follow him, leaving a good measure of space between them, and wherever Tristan went, Alexa wasn't far away. This continued for weeks until Mindy found out, then she sent Austin and Liam to keep a close eye on them, and soon enough Jax knew he wasn't getting the solitude he longed for, this then resulted in Mindy ensuring Jax had something more than just four walls. He was the first to have a fridge and washing machine which became a trend and trickled all throughout the village.

Mindy was happy, the laundry room in the shelter wasn't being abused by frustrated werewolves and the guys were happy they didn't have to haul bags of dirty clothes through the snow back and forth.

Everything ran on solar, which wasn't always in our favor. We had set up in a part of the world that was often cloudy, so use was restricted to once a fortnight for everyone. The shelter ran on generators, so every monthly trip to Kamloops also meant a big fuel run.

But restock days were happy ones. Mindy would toot the horn half a mile away and we knew it was cold hotdogs, pizzas, and on a lucky day, poutine.

The early days were great, it was more of a family vibe, everyone chipped in to put supplies away, everyone looked out for Tristan and Alexa, and we all took it in turns checking in on Jax. It took him a good year to overcome his grief and come out on a more frequent basis, but he was never the same after Kyle.

Carrie and Ezra kept their distance from one another after Kyle's death. She kept herself busy finding ways to make the Precinct self-sufficient but there were never enough resources or humans to maintain it.

Full moons were a full lockdown for us humans, we sealed the shelter at midday and the howls over the next twenty-four hours were a torment. Sometimes it was so loud it shook the foundations; we always heard fighting. Tears we constantly flowing as we worried who'd be left at the door with injuries and that one day if those injuries would be too far gone. It was never safe here; we all knew if they wanted to get it, they would.

In truth life at the Precinct was a life sentence, once you were here it was hard to leave, but if you left— you would never be the same again.

I remember everything so vividly, it never faded.

V.J.Garland

CHAPTER TWO

JAX

Present Day

It's been years since we opened the bunker and made a home here at Willmore. The fields are full of cabins now and those cabins are full of werewolves, the more cabins the closer in proximity they became, and soon it was a village—affectionately known as Wolftown.

Most werewolves were in *almost* complete control. Word had spread through Austin, Liam, and Ezra's connections of a sanctuary for anyone who wished to try and regain their former selves.

Christian and Arthur rebuilt a prison transfer vehicle and began picking up wolves in nearby areas, some with families who also came to stay at the bunker. Though for most of us that was already a missed opportunity, they'd either mauled their way through their homes or they'd chased them off.

Most families that came didn't stay for long, living at the Precinct was grim and many of the humans had a hard time getting through the full moons. Full moons were the one day a month we were unable to control our transformations, the weaker of the wolves were less reliable, they would randomly erupt in fur and fangs at the slightest trigger — anger, hunger, the list was ongoing, and at any given moment.

After Kyle's passing, Carrie took it upon herself to ensure everyone's safety, she would meet with me weekly to go over ideas and relayed them as my own to ensure I maintained control over the Precinct, she understood the importance of having a solid union between the original residents and the newcomers.

Jensen and Reggie were the first to join us. They had come all the way from Europe, crossing through Eastern Russia, catching a boat to Diomede's, another to Wales and then spending months hunting their way down Alaska and finally to Willmore. Word had spread much wider than I ever anticipated.

In the first months, as we found our footing, so many of the women here were scratched during brawls that broke out, often over food. Every injury was cleaned and healed, and no repercussions ever followed. There were no casualties, not even for the wolves.

We had been lucky—so far.

My cabin was outside of Wolftown, on the outer perimeter where I could watch from a distance and maintain my privacy. I left for nothing and so Carrie and Mindy had Arthur build a tiny little kitchen into my cabin and eventually expanded my laundry space into a small bathroom, so I wasn't bathing in the river anymore.

For the first few months while I revelled in my grief Izzy and Celinde would take a walk through Wolftown and deliver me Mindy's homecooked meals, some frozen. That was before the Precinct took in more occupants. There were too many close calls with new settlers for them to check in as often as they had once done.

Suddenly Lupina's freezer made sense to me, it was hard enough getting out of bed, or peeling myself from the sofa, let alone cooking an actual meal. I was no stranger to cooking, but I couldn't recall the last time I cooked for one. It was always me and Lupe or Joel.

It was the same cycle day in, and day out. I'd wake up and peer out of my window as I drank down burnt instant coffee, I'd eat a Costco cookie that Mindy included in my fortnightly delivery, then sit down in front of the fireplace and watch a movie picked from an old leather DVD case that Alexa found in the bunker. I'd usually have a peanut butter and jelly sandwich for lunch and then frozen mac and cheese or something of the variety for dinner.

Tristan tried leaving fresh kills on my porch every so often—I wouldn't touch them.

I'd never touch a raw carcass or body again after what I'd done. The recollection of what happened on Cannon Beach was fresh in my mind even years on and would be for a long time to come.

For what I was and the power I held my existence felt bleak. I knew I could be living in far less squaller than I was. I didn't need to chain myself up every full moon, I could run free and bound across the acreage and mountaintops like the rest of them, but I simply didn't trust myself anymore.

Neither did they though, and I didn't blame them. I'd committed more crimes against my friends than strangers, everyone I'd harmed had some meaning to someone here. I longed for the days of white corridors, cold coffee, and patients being hauled in with fishing hooks through their lips or old guys dislocating their shoulders with a bad line cast. This was hell and I was Fenrir, evil was the extent of any expectancy of me now.

My comforts were chains, ways to keep me subdued and content; to make sure I didn't wreak havoc once more.

There were other cabins out here, but they were old and made from moldy materials, they didn't last. In effect my *neighborhood* looked somewhat daunting, abandoned, and often became a punching bag, it's where the others came to let off steam by smashing windows or hurling one another through logs — anything went on a full moon and no grudges were held.

V.J.Garland

CHAPTER THREE

THEN LUCY

HAPPENED...

The wind was violent, waging an assault of icy blades against Lucy's frosty, blushed cheeks. Her car was inoperable and the heat from the exasperated heating system was quickly escaping into the mist of snow through the open door.

Lucy kicked the front wheel in a fit of anger, she'd spent the weekend in a soup kitchen fifty miles away from her hometown. She'd taken the backroads home, the GPS navigation system telling her it would be 20mins faster.

But she was stuck on what was once a gravel road three feet deep in snow and growing with a stalled run-down old car. She was fresh out of college and bouncing between volunteer work to make her resume more appealing after failing to hold down a paying job.

Night was only hours away and there was no sign of civilization around—She'd have to walk or freeze in the car.

She dragged herself through the snow, the only sign of the road being the open field of white not laced with pine trees above it. No phone reception, and not even a powerline is in sight. She took her backpack from the weekend stay at the shelter and left the car unlocked to avoid vandals smashing the windows. The car was old and on its final legs, nothing of value in it except to be used for parts if it couldn't be revived.

She forced her frozen limbs through the powder-filled road for hours, suddenly she spotted old log cabins, some without rooves others boasting smashed windows—No good for sheltering in. There were no street signs with hopes of towns any distance away. She had wandered too far off the main road now. She trudged through a little longer and the sun began to disappear as the moon peaked its brightness out and illuminated the white talc that now clung to her black pants.

A small glimmer of light blinked in the distance beneath the cover of trees, and she forced her last ounce of energy toward it, her legs felt frozen, the adrenaline taking hold as she sprinted like a rabbit over the insidious, yet beautiful fluffy pasture.

She arrived at a small log cabin, this one was intact, there were curtains over the windows but stained with browned notes of age, likely never washed. The door was large and heavy, and she hammered her fists down on it before collapsing on the small deck.

Moments passed and the door creaked open. Jax appeared. He stood mystified in the doorway looking over the unconscious woman who lay on his small porch. Jax collected her in his arms and peered around the field before bringing her inside. The cabin was dimly lit with a fireplace burning in one corner, a small kitchen to one end, and in the far corner a messy bed with old checked woollen blankets swathed over the bedpost.

He laid her on the old lounge in front of the fire and removed her soaking wet boots and placed them in front of the fireplace to dry.

Jax was a man of few words, he had deep mesmerizing eyes, with a rough, tired look about him. The kind of look that tells you he didn't care about much, even less his appearance. He had a shaggy overgrown beard, oily overgrown hair about four inches in length, and clothes that looked more like rags.

He placed a small table beside the sofa with a peanut butter sandwich, an apple and a glass of water encase she woke hungry. He dumped the knife into the sink which already overflowed onto the small bench space. Jax searched for a dry towel and a spare shirt knowing she would want to change. Finally, he lay a warm blanket over her before he retired to the bed far earlier than he had anticipated.

Jax was less than pleased with the invasion of his privacy, he lived a quiet life most of the time unless Carrie or Mindy came around with food or to complain. It was common for Christian and Ezra to visit but rarely others.

Morning broke and the light drifted in through a hole in the curtain waking Lucy first. The fireplace had faded as the last log burnt out and Lucy tore off her damp pants. She sat up on the lounge looking around unsure of where she was. There was only one door in the cabin which led to what she assumed to be a bathroom and she quietly tiptoed towards it before looking around the cozy little cabin. She ran the hot water and sat on the floor of the shower drinking in the steam as it warmed her half-blue body. As she looked about the room, she saw a washing machine and dryer beside the basin next to a small bathtub filled with dirty clothes.

"Ugh, this person is a slob!" she gushed in disgust quietly to herself.

Cautious not to spend too much time in a stranger's bathroom, she reluctantly turned off the hot water and wrapped herself in the single damp-smelling towel. She pulled the long-sleeved flannelette top over her head avoiding the buttons and dumped her clothes and a bunch from the bathtub into the empty washing machine, filled it with powder, and set the cycle to heavy duty.

She tiptoed once more out of the bathroom and past the snoring that came from the bed. She peered over to see Jax sound asleep wrapped cosily in the big bed.

There was a small TV with nothing but a DVD player, and a massive action collection, some horrors, and documentaries. Lucy was more of a Rom-com girl and nothing much took her fancy. She chucked on a movie for some background noise while she ate the now stale sandwich. The lounge was a little wet from her pants and she removed the covers and took them to the dryer.

Once that was taken care of, she decided the least she could do was tackle the pile of dirty dishes. She fumbled around searching for a sponge and detergent and emptied the sink as quietly as she could and ran the hot water. Jax was waking in the distance—thrilled to hear the dishes being washed.

Lucy scrubbed through dish after dish and fork after fork until the bench was covered in clean cutlery and plates. She began to rinse the soap from them, and Jax appeared behind her with a single dry tea towel.

"You didn't have to..." he sighed with embarrassment.

"It's the least I could do, I don't even remember coming inside," she sighed.

"You were passed out," he replied.

"Thank you," she smiled.

He nodded and continued through the dishes, putting them away as he went.

Lucy turned back to the sink and finished rinsing just in time for the beepers to go on the washer and dryer. She took aim and beelined away from the awkwardness and into the bathroom, unloaded the dryer and washer, and filled the dryer with freshly washed clothes. Then took the sofa cover back out and recovered the cushions.

"Hope you don't mind. I did some washing," she said as she fumbled over the cushions.

"You didn't have to," Jax said through a forced smile.

Yes, I did... she thought to herself.

As she peered around the cabin she was only welcomed by the mess, the kitchen was finally clear, but the rest of the place made her feel claustrophobic.

"I'm going for my morning run..." Jax lied as he quickly closed the door behind him.

"But the snow!" Lucy called out, but it was too late—He was gone.

Still hungry she opened the fridge and pulled out a packet of bacon, milk, butter, and eggs. There was flour in the cupboard, and she whipped up a pancake batter to have with the bacon.

An hour passed and she had devoured her plate of food and left a plate for Jax, whose name she still didn't know.

She sat on the sofa once more, this time with the pile of warm clean clothes, and began folding them all as she ignored the horror movie playing in the background.
Five shirts in and the front door swung open and Jax poured in—covered in sweat.

Lucy turned to make eye contact, but Jax was pressed over the bench with his back towards her. He wiped away a trace of blood from his forehead careful not to show her as his face healed from his transformation.
"Thanks for the food," he said as he rushed into the bathroom.

"You're welcome..." but the bathroom door slammed cutting off her sentence.

In the bathroom he observed the washing machine running once again and the bathtub was finally empty for the first time in months. He peered into the mirror where his face was still healing after being struck by Graham.

Jax's leadership of the Precinct was known but as newcomers flowed in, the more his status was challenged. Graham was the latest obstacle.

With the towel wrapped around his waist, he left the bathroom and spied the stack of clean warm folded clothes on Lucy's lap as she battled through the messy pile beside her.

"May I?" he asked as he hovered over her folding up her pants.

"Sure," She smiled as she tucked her pants beside her and handed him his mound of clothing.

He walked off back to the bathroom, but she yelled out to stop him.

"Wait! I don't even know your name?" she questioned.
"Jax... you are?" he asked.

"Lucy," She replied.
He nodded and kept walking toward the bathroom to change into his fresh clothing.

The clothes were finally folded, and Lucy stood up to stretch and then grabbed all the dirty towels she had spotted while folding. She raced around to collect them and threw them into the washing machine still miffed at the mess Jax lived in.

He was sprawled over the bed with a book in hand, his eyes locked with hers for the first time and a small smile escaped him. She had long wavy dark locks, hazel eyes a pale complexion, rosy lips, and a bright enchanting smile. She had another basket of dried linens in her arms and lugged them over to her newfound base, the lounge.

For the first time he had *seen* her, not just felt a presence. Jax sat up in his bed and watched over her as she tidied about his tiny home. He was intrigued by her motivation to declutter and clean from top to bottom.
He felt the urge to address her situation. He knew he had made no effort to assist or even discover what it was that lead her here and just how bad it may have been if she knocked on the wrong cabin. He was quick to blame the others, convinced it was a setup to make him feed on her.

"What brings you here?" he asked as he motioned closer to the fireplace in front of her.

"My car broke down a few miles away," She sighed.

"So, you walked here?" he muttered.

"Yep!" she said shortly, she was unamused that he had taken so long to ask for this information.

He hovered about picking up items that had laid in place for months. Things that didn't belong on a coffee table, old boots, a mug with old tea that was growing something with a foul odor.

"I'll take care of that," Lucy stood up and took the mug from his hand. He towered over her as they got too close.

"You really don't have to," He sighed with embarrassment.

"I'd like to," With that, she sprung off to the kitchen, emptied the contents, and soaked it in a tub of boiling water from the kettle. Jax wasn't far behind her with an arm full of more dirty dishes he'd found lying around.

"Would you mind if I cooked dinner?" Lucy asked.

Jax's ears pricked up with excitement.

"Anything but frozen meals," He chuffed with a smile.

"Great, what do we have?" she asked.

Jax dove into the fridge and retrieved a bird gutted and feathered.

"You killed this?" she asked.

"Yep," He replied.

"Impressive… any garlic, onions?" she questioned.

"Just have a look around. You've already made yourself at home," he snickered.

"Sorry, I don't mean to be like this. I felt as though I owed you one for taking me in," she sighed.

"I didn't mean it like that, it's nice having someone here getting it all done," He let a smile slip.

"Do you like stuffing?" she asked.

"Always!" he said enthused.

"Great!" Lucy began chopping vegetables and mixing stuffing made from an old loaf of bread while Jax put a movie on and sat on the sofa pretending to fold the linen.

Hours passed and Lucy had snuck off to shed the bedding and wash it all and dry it before dinner.
The clock hit 8 pm and she could hear her stomach eating itself as Jax pulled the roasting racks from the oven.
A perfect golden chicken with buttery stuffing and a generous assortment of vegetables and gravy.

"It's been so long since I had freshly cooked food...well aside from the microwave," Jax confessed.

"Why?" she asked confused.

He avoided the question and lowered his head only distracted by the smells wafting before his face.
"It's hard to explain," He replied as he pulled out a knife to begin carving.

Lucy brought over two plates and began dishing up the food for them both. They sat together on the sofa and ate quietly, only occasionally lifting their eyes to one another. His expressions were of satisfaction and enjoyment, hers of curiosity and lust. He was a tall attractive man, with messy hair, a messy beard, and a chest of sparse hair that poorly hid his definition.

"Thank you for dinner," He smiled as he got up to serve himself seconds.

"My pleasure," She smiled as she got up to fit the bed with the now dry linen.

"Mind if I take this pillow?" she asked as she reached for one of the four on the bed.

"Just sleep here tonight, no need to sleep on that uncomfortable sofa," he smiled.

"No funny business…" he quickly retorted.

"You're sure?" Lucy asked.

"I'm not trying to put moves on you, I promise," He assured her.

"Okay," She agreed.

She fluffed the pillows and took the side not pressed to the wall. Jax turned off the lights as he finished his food so she could get some sleep. He packed the remaining food into old containers and rinsed off the roasting pans before taking some time to pace in front of the fireplace. From time to time, he tossed logs into the fire to keep the warmth flowing throughout the cabin.

There were noises outside. Noises he recognized, he took his coat and went outside to investigate.

"What do you want Graham?" he grunted at the shadow in the distance.

"Just make sure your snack is out of here tomorrow, you know what could happen to wanderers around here…" he teased.

"Her car broke down, no need to threaten her," Jax scowled.

"Wasn't saying I'd do it; you'll be close enough to take care of it yourself," He laughed.

Jax grew wild with anger and raced toward Graham with fangs bared and claws ready to strike.

"See, you can't even take a little friendly advice Jax, these are your own rules," Graham scoffed smugly.

"Get out of here before I end you," his forehead met Graham's as his rage escalated.

The tension was high and several more shadows appeared, two behind Jax, more behind Graham.

"Let it go..." one urged as he grabbed Jax and pulled him away from the confrontation.
Graham disappeared with a blink shortly followed by the others.

"Sit down!" Jamal demanded.

Jax listened and sat in the snow beside the two men.

One was goofy and joking around pretending to air punch in Graham's direction. He had curly red hair and bright yellow eyes, fangs protruding only to rip the lid from a bottle of beer from a six-pack he carried in hand. He tossed the open beer to Jax as it slightly spilled down his chest—It was Liam.

"Moron!" Jax laughed.

"You know he's right though. She can't stay here, not in the village," said the more sensible of the two. Jamal was of African descent, with the same yellow eyes as Liam, fangs also bared as if this were his normal state.

"I know she can't," he sighed.

"Don't do that... don't get attached. Have your fun with her and send her on her way, it's the only way, or you could eat her..." Liam suggested in a sexual tone.

"I'm not going to do that," He scoffed unamused.

"Well get her on her way—tomorrow," Jamal urged.

"There's still time before the full moon," Jax argued.

"It's in your hands, you're the boss around here. I trust you to make the right decision," Liam clinked his bottle with Jax' and Jamal's and quickly disappeared in the same blink of time.

"Goodnight, Jax," Jamal smiled.

"Goodnight, Jamal," Jax sighed as he chugged the remainder of the beer.

He paced slowly back to the cabin. It had been a long time since he had had any meaningful relationships with a human and Lucy just felt special to him. She had a warmth about her that made him forget his horrors. He felt like a human with her, he was able to restrain his inner beast. A distraction he desperately needed.

He entered the cabin, Lucy lightly snoring on the bed curled up in his flannelette shirt, the buttons popping open down to her navel, he removed his clothes, all but his underwear, and climbed over the top of her into his side of the bed. She squirmed about from the disturbance and lay her head on his arm. All the warning signs told him to pull away, but he rolled her into him and wrapped his big arms around her. Jax didn't sleep a wink that night. Instead staring deep into Lucy's face and playing with soft bouncy tresses of hair that covered her eyes.

Morning broke and Lucy began to squirm once more, and Jax quickly pretended to be asleep. Her eyes flickered open as she began to gather some sense of where she was once more. He expected her to bound out of bed in protest to their entanglement, but she wriggled in a little closer and placed her hand on his chest, and tried to sleep a little more. His arms tightened and his lips pressed against her forehead. Her leg slipped between his as she opened her eyes to stroke his cheek.

"Are you awake?" she whispered gently.

"Barely…" he whispered back.

He stroked her back as he looked deeply into her porcelain face pulling her to him and pressing himself into her ruby-red lips.

"We shouldn't," he sighed through an almost kiss.
"But it feels right," She smiled.

"I'm not good for your well-being," He confessed.

"My well-being?" Lucy's horny left immediately and was replaced with doubts and concerns.

"It's not safe for you here? you need to leave…" he answered.

Lucy climbed out of the bed embarrassed and quickly pulled her clothes on.

"Not right now!" he scoffed.

"It's better if I just leave…I'm sorry, this isn't what I came here for," she sighed in shame.

"Your car is still broken," Jax added.

"Yes, it is. I'll figure it out," She grabbed her bag and left the cabin, and began trudging through the thick powder once again.

She half expected Jax to follow her, but she knew he was simpler than that, her drama wasn't hers and the likely reason he lived away from civilization. His cares and worries were few. She followed the white field for hours in the direction she had come from and after several miles stumbled upon her car almost buried in snow.

"Fuck!" she screamed.

"I'm going to die here"… she grumbled to herself.

She shoveled snow away with her hands. She tried to wrench the door open, but the snow was too deep and compacted. She accepted defeat and climbed up on top of the car and lay on the roof. It was cold and the sun did little to warm her. Several hours passed, and a figure appeared in the distance, slowly getting closer and closer. She closed her eyes and suddenly she was ripped from the roof of the car.

"Do you have any idea how long I've been looking for you," Jax scowled.

"You told me to leave!" she screamed back.

"No! you said it was better if you left, I didn't agree," He fought back.

Jax tossed her over his shoulder and moved over the ice with no struggle at all.

"How are you doing that?" she asked still angry.

"I told you it's for your own well-being…" he began. "Blah blah blah…" she cut him off and he ignored any conversation for the miles to come.

They reached the porch of the cabin and Jax dumped her down roughly.

"Ouch!" she yelled.

"Serves you right," He yelled back.

"Why did you even come after me?" she sulked.

"Because there are more dishes to be done," He joked sarcastically.

She screwed up a snowball and threw it directly at his face. The talc shattered and his beard became white with snow.

"I'm sorry," she said quickly with regret as he launched a handful of snow at her.

"Too late!" Jax laughed.

She was already molding large handfuls of snow in retaliation.

"A lot of noise, Jax," Graham approached.

"Sorry, I didn't know anyone else lived close by," Lucy smiled, and she went to shake his hand.

Jax quickly threw himself in front of her and knocked her to the ground.

"That's no way to treat a lady!" Graham interjected.
"I know how you'd like to treat ladies..." Jax scowled.
His fangs were out once more and his eyes became a violent shade of red.

"What are you doing here?" Jax demanded.

"Just watching over the neighborhood," he said teasingly as he gawked at Lucy, he licked the air to savor her scent.

Jax's back was facing Lucy as she backed slowly toward the cabin sensing his displeasure at Graham's presence. His expression became wilder the more Graham pressed him. His hands began to morph slowly, first, the claws forced out his human nails, they dropped to the snow with blobs of blood making them obvious in the white cloud. Graham sneered as Lucy turned and was faced with more of the men. One grabbed her viciously and forced her to observe the rage that embodied Jax. His body grew in anger, his face broke in four as a muzzle appeared, wiry hair materialized and soon all signs of clothes were nothing but shreds on the ground.

Graham had his way and Lucy was a blubbering mess wondering what world she had stumbled into. Jax launched at Graham, his retaliation was faster, his transformation effortless and timely, unlike Jax's slow mutation. Graham was old, far older than Jax, even Ezra.

They wrestled about in the snow for several minutes, yelps and roars often heard as claws full, and mouthfuls of hair and flesh flew about the open field. Evan had her by the throat forcing her to watch on as they fought.

She struggled to get away but knew it was worthless.

Four more wolves leaped down from a hill that had a towering spotlight beaming now at the fight tearing through the snow.

"JAX," Christian yelled.

Christian raced down into the open valley and threw himself into the midst of the fight, Jamal and Tristan tried to wrestle Graham to the ground. The field was now full of yellow eyes. Carrie and Celinde raced down the hill and dragged themselves through the snow, arriving puffed and weary.

The girls shot glares at Evan to release Lucy and they stood beside her and tried to calm her as they brought her back into Jax's cabin.

Arthur and Henry came down next with chains, shackles, and sealed buckets full of colloidal silver and rope ready to be saturated.

"Bring him to his cabin," Arthur sighed to Tristan. Tristan and Jamal had their claws buried into Graham's shoulder blades forcing him to move as they directed.

"Carrie! We need you…" Arthur called out.

Celinde nodded at Carrie as she sat with Lucy.
Mindy made her way down as soon as Arthur was out of sight, and she did her best to bounce through the snow like an excitable bunny.
She lunged for the patio and managed not to spill any part of her basket of grocery goods.

Jax was still laying in the snow, slowly changing back. A good sign that he'd heal but no time soon.

"Celinde!" Mindy called as she pushed through the front door.

"Oh! I saw you from the bunker, I'm glad you're okay," she kneeled before Lucy and rubbed her hand.

"This is Mindy," Celinde smiled.

"Is everyone here like that," Lucy said, still in a state of shock as she pulled her hands away from Mindy, reluctant to touch her.

"No, just the men," Mindy explained.

"Come up to the bunker, it'll be safer for you in there," Celinde encouraged as she packed away the food Mindy had brought down.

"What about him? is he going to be, okay?" Lucy asked as she stared out through the open door at Jax's body. It began jerking back and forth as he regained consciousness.

"Jax! He'll be fine, Graham would never kill him," Celinde laughed.

"How can you be certain?" Lucy questioned.

"He's the big dog, if Jax dies, so do they. This stuff happens occasionally; new people come, and they try and live our lifestyle for a while, but most disappear before we can serve them pancakes, it's not for everyone. Jax learned to stop chasing after all the bad guys a long time ago," Celinde explained.

"Granted, Graham's swarm has lasted the longest," Mindy grunted.

"Swarm!" Celinde snickered.

"That's what they are! Pests, insects, I don't like how Evan's eyes chase after Alexa," Mindy growled.

"Nothing will ever come of it. Alexa has eyes for Tristan, and now that she's old enough..." Celinde teased.

"I'm going to smack the words clean out of your mouth if you continue that sentence, Ms. Maxwell!" Mindy croaked.

Lucy was still frozen on the sofa, grasping at her thoughts, and glancing into the fireplace through the steam that warmed her lips from the hot cup of tea.

"She should probably eat something..." Mindy glanced over.

"I'll warm up a Jax special," Celinde nodded.

Celinde pulled out a frozen lasagna from the freezer and tossed it into the microwave and set the timer.

Six years ago, Jax wouldn't be caught dead with a frozen dinner in his house, he mocked Lupina repeatedly for having so many filling her freezer, but now he had fallen into the same terrible cycle he had pulled her out of.

"Why so much lasagna?" Celinde asked as she searched through the freezer.

"That's just what he asks for on his list he sends up every fortnight," Mindy shrugged her shoulders.

"Oh, and instant ramen, and then they get all their usual stuff," Mindy smiled proudly.

Mindy and Izzy had the grocery picking down to a fine art. Austin and Alexa had the greenhouse at full capacity growing all the necessities from greenhouse towers. Tomatoes, potatoes, carrots, onions, bell peppers, lettuce, and strawberries. There was a whole family room dedicated to chickens, so they had a constant supply of fresh eggs, but it was never enough, they always ran out of eggs.

Mindy would organize a fortnight supply of food, including eggs, milk, bread, a hot roast chicken, bacon, and a variety of meat, fruit, and vegetables. Monthly they would receive another package of flour, rice, sugar, tea, coffee, and anything else that might need restocking.

Some came to the bunker to collect their goods; others had a neighbor drop them off.

A lot of the wolves lived a life of solitude. Many chose to stay as part of the brotherhood but were allowed the freedom to roam and hunt as they pleased, but anyone caught breaking the rules was swiftly and brutally punished and made an example of publicly in the town center.

Some hunted for the bunker, and Carrie would give orders for what she desired. This was usually fulfilled by Tristan.

Tristan never lost the urge to hunt, and he adapted well to hunting for animals. Alexa would sneak out and watch him some days. She always had eyes for Tristan and had shadowed his every move since she developed an attraction to him. Alexa had blossomed into a natural beauty, but Tristan knew Mindy and Arthur would never let him touch her, so he focused on his duties and obeyed every word Jax said like it was scripture.

Lucy became pale as she watched Jax sit up in the snow as his face reanimated right before her from the open window.

She fell from the sofa to her knees and spilled her tea. Her stomach bubbled as the last of the color left her face and she heaved over and involuntarily vomited all over herself. Jax stumbled his way inside to her as best he could. Mindy came over seconds later with a mug of warm water and a blanket that she gently wrapped around her.

"Let's get you up to the shelter and find you a way home..." Mindy smiled.
Jax picked her up and carried her all the way through the muddy snow and up the hill to the bunker door, she went in silence without objection, Celinde was puffing behind them.

"Are you okay?" Jax laughed.

"I hate that walk with a passion," she exhaled.

"That's why you stopped visiting Christian?" He murmured.

"That's not up for discussion, Jax," Celinde snapped.
Alexa opened the doors with Izzy and helped Lucy inside.

"Are you coming?" Lucy asked as Jax stood outside in the red ambiance.

He hung his head sadly and spun on his heel and walked back towards the path.

Celinde glared as Jax hesitated and took one final glance behind him as Lucy disappeared into the shelter.

"What are you doing?" Celinde asked.

"Thinking... with two minds," he sighed.

"Be very careful with what you do next, what's good for you, isn't necessarily good for her," Celinde glowered.

Christian appeared from the path with Ezra, Jake, and Tristan as they hauled the latest catch-up to the shelter.

The mood was eerie and once Celinde cast her eyes on Christian there was an obvious tension in the air.

"I'll leave..." Christian sighed.

"What is going on?" Jax questioned.

"Bad break-up, that's all I can say for it," Jake began.

"You guys broke up?" Jax gasped.

"Where have you been, Jax?" Celinde scowled.

She had bred obvious hate for the wolves, her appearance was dull, and she oozed fear even though she tried desperately not to show it.

"Maybe you should go with Lucy...Wherever that may be," Jax suggested.

"You want to send me away?" She yelled.

"Celinde, you're not okay. Not anymore, if you want to come back when you're feeling more yourself you can, but you need a break," Christian sighed as he moved closer to her.

"I can't leave Carrie..." she wept.

Jax looked around at those closest to him and threw the doors to the shelter open and entered for the first time in a long time.

"Everyone, get out here now!" He yelled.
Mindy, Izzy, Alexa, Carrie, and Lucy all emerged from the kitchen, all paler in appearance, tired beyond the help of sleep, and in desperate need of vitamin D.

"Is everything okay?" Carrie asked.

"You're all going on a holiday," Jax began.

"I'm sorry what?" Alexa interrupted as she rushed to Tristan and clung to his arm tightly.

"If you don't want to come back, that's okay too," Jax sighed.

"This isn't your problem anymore, we won't recover, or age, you are wasting your lives with us," Ezra added.

"What the fuck, Ezra!" Carrie snapped.

"You know it's true, I can't even sleep in the same bed as you, that's no relationship…" he sighed.

Lucy's eyes pricked up and locked with Jax's. She walked towards him, gripped his arm, and forced him to walk down to a quiet room while the others were left to make assumptions of their own.

"He's been hiding her in his cabin…" Graham entered the shelter spitting his venomous words, grabbing the attention of those who would listen.

"Jax would never do that!" Carrie objected.

"Are you so sure? He's a recluse! We never see him…" Graham's words were dangerous.

"You don't know what you're talking about old man," Tristan growled in Jax's defense.

"I know I've been here six months and he's come out of his cabin twice. Once to enforce his power and the second to fight me over his pet," Graham growled.

"Then leave...nobody is keeping you here," Alexa snarled.

Tristan forced her back behind him, but Graham slid closer as he sniffed the air she occupied seconds before. Arthur filled the space between Tristan and Graham and made himself bigger, his teeth were ravenous and his claws sharper.

"Dad!" Alexa squealed.

"Don't fight the big bad wolf, Daddy," Graham teased, his eyes darkened to their deep shade of Orange and his cheekbones cracked with unnatural ease.

"Take it outside!" Celinde ordered with a screech.

She was on the brink of a mental breakdown; she tore at her face and hair then dropped to the ground trying to block her ears from the sound of murder that broke out as every wolf marched up to the shelter from the village.

"What is happening?" Lucy asked as she peered around the corner, Jax right behind her.

"Get in the Jeep! NOW!" Jax ordered as he pointed to all the women.

"There's not enough room!" Alexa objected.

"MAKE ROOM!" Jax growled.

Lucy grabbed Jax and hugged him goodbye as he gently brushed her cheek.

"You are so much more than the bad things that happen to you," she whispered as she kissed him gently and he held her with hopelessness.

The women crammed themselves into the crowded Jeep with four more in the boot and nobody brave enough to drive or sit up front.

"Tristan, Ezra... Get them somewhere safe!" Jax pushed them inside and held Lucy's eyes in his for as long as he could.

Ezra sped them off down the snow-covered road, plowing through as fast as he could.

"That won't be enough," Clarence smiled.

Otis and Jamal leaped through the mess hall and tackled Graham and Clarence to the ground and tied them up once again.

"You know this doesn't work, right?" Jamal muttered.

"Austin, can you and Liam follow them, make sure they are safe," Jax asked.

"Of course," Austin grabbed Jax's shoulder and pressed his forehead to Jax's in their brotherly way.

Jax still commanded a great deal of respect, he had a bond with everyone here and he smelt trouble the minute it landed on his doorstep.

V.J.Garland

Chapter Four

Carrie

I knew I shouldn't second guess myself by now, but I still couldn't believe how quickly a situation like that could escalate in a blip. Celinde and Christian hadn't told anyone about their separation. She'd been numb for months, if not years now. I never thought to ask, I thought Christian was her happy place, the way Ezra was for me.

It was a cruel way to have found love— for all of us.

She never made eye contact with any of us for the hours it took to reach Kamloops.

"You all just need to take a few days, soak in a sauna, and eat up some good food!" Izzy smiled as she hugged Celinde from sitting beside her.

"There'll be someone else one day…" Celinde sighed.

"Well, you never love the same way twice, you know it's real when it hurts," Izzy added as she rubbed Celinde's back.

"Does it hurt for you?" Celinde asked.

"It hurts to see Henry struggle with an anomaly in his body, something wildly out of his own control. It doesn't feel the same anymore, but it's what's familiar to me," she explained.

"So, you stay out of habit?" Ezra asked.

"There's nothing for any of us at Wolftown, Ezra…" Izzy replied.

"There's just hopes and dreams that we'll all wake up back in Cannon Beach one morning and this was a bad nightmare," Mindy added.

"Can someone please tell me what the hell is happening," Lucy begged.

"Werewolves…" Alexa replied.

"Werewolves? Like fictional shifter werewolves?" she asked.

"Like, can carve you open before you've even blinked, werewolves," Celinde added.

"That's not very encouraging…" Lucy huffed.

"What do you want me to tell you, Lucy? That Jax will be your turning point romance? That your instant connection is revolutionary and that you have a future at

Wolftown, and you'll have a werewolf wedding and little werewolf babies?" Celinde began to unload her rage.

"Celinde!" I growled.
"No! you're the worst of them, Carrie!" I shut up and accepted defeat. I knew she was right.

I'd spent my every waking hour making sure the village was habitable for the wolves and that everything ran smoothly for them. Jax never knew we ran out of food some winters and we girls lived on rotting vegetables. It was too important to keep *them* all fed, if they weren't fed, we were the next meal, regardless of whether they wanted to or not. My entire existence thrived on being needed. I was good in a jam; I was resourceful and assertive enough to make sure my bidding was done.

Jax wasn't the monster— it was me. I took control, in his name, and did what was needed to see the Precinct survive.

At the end of every day, I was ensuring the well-being and safety of the wrong race. I was a traitor to the women around me.

"We're here," Tristan exclaimed with a sigh of relief.

"Finally!" Izzy scrambled out of the car as fast as she could.

"That was painful," Ezra smiled as he rubbed my shoulder.

I shrugged him off and chased after Celinde, a warning not to follow me.

"Where's home for you, Lucy?" I asked as she skipped alongside me.

"Hinton," she replied.

"Oh, where were you coming from when you came across Jax?" I questioned.

"McBride," she replied once more.

"Bet you wish you stayed home," Celinde chimed as she scrunched her eyebrows.

"Look, I'm sorry, but how long were you happy before you were miserable?" She asserted Celinde.

Celinde smiled a real smile, and a rebellious tear betrayed her stronger-than-usual stance.

"Maybe you aren't so bad…" Celinde brushed her hair mousey hair off her face and granted Lucy a smile and gentle nod as the words touched her, and thoughts rushed through her mind.

Celinde walked faster and caught up with Mindy while I hung back with Lucy.

"It's been hard for her, hasn't it?" Lucy asked.

"Extremely…" I answered.

"We can take you home in a few days, after everyone's caught their breath," I offered.

"Is your boyfriend going back?" She asked.

"To the Precinct? I hope not," I sighed.

"That's where he belongs though isn't it?" she asked.

"At this point, I feel like all human werewolf relationships are null and void, he can do whatever he wants," I said reluctantly.

Curiosity peaked and I could feel her anxiety about wanting to return to the Precinct.

"How long were you down there with him?" I asked.

"Only a few days, he saved my life," she explained.

"I know you're young and Jax is dangerous, ruggedly handsome, and it's all exciting, but you don't want that life. Even if you thought you could make it work, you couldn't," I pressed my lips together as we sat down on a bed in a quiet small room.

"How can you be so sure?" She quizzed.

"In the jeep, there's a diary, it's Lupe's. She tried for five years," I started.

"Where is she now?" Lucy asked.

"She's dead, her husband killed her," I explained.

"Tell it properly!" Celinde interrupted from the door.

"You're far more tender than I know how to be...why don't you," I smiled at her.

Celinde took in a deep breath as she began to recount the anarchy Lupe endured in her five years with Noah, she explained how Christian lost himself to preserve Noah's memory and how Jax had been caught up in the crossfire trying to save Lupina.

Lucy drank in every word and felt every emotion like it was her own and I felt her sweet young heart shatter for Jax.

"He's lost everything, and you all expect him to just be okay, alone…forever?" Lucy questioned.

This puzzled me, it puzzled me because of how much sense it made. Lucy was right, we all just expected him to carry on through his grief and never feel happiness again, just protecting everyone else, holding down the Precinct at his own expense.

"You like him?" Celinde smiled.

"I do," Lucy admitted.

"We knew Jax before the onset. He was a wonderful person, before this life before he lost Joel, Kyle, and Lupe. He's still in there, if you want to try, we won't stop you…" Celinde sighed.

"Okay, madam nostalgia over here is a quick sway. You will die if you go back there, you can't be turned, they don't age, there's no future. Walk away while you can," I urged.

Celinde had that glimmer in her eyes, the one I had missed that made her special. Lucy had awoken a side of her that I couldn't.
"I'll sleep on it. You guys have been through it, I'll consider your advice, from both sides," she agreed.

"I'm going to go check on Tristan," I sighed.

"Maybe you should check on Ezra instead," Celinde groaned.

I left the room without responding, I didn't want to get into it with her over Ezra. But there he was, curled up on a recliner at the end of the hallway half asleep with a bottle of iced coffee in his lap. I walked towards him and took a sip from the bottle and sat on the ground beside his chair while he ran his fingers through my messy curls.

"I'm sorry…" I whispered.

"It's okay, this is a lot to deal with. Austin and Liam just arrived, I'll bunk with them," he stood up and pulled me up by my hands.

"Ez…" I lost my words.

"It's okay, we knew at some point this would reach an expiration date," he sighed.

"I'm sorry," I whispered again.

He pressed my hands together gently, kissed my messy hair, and raced off down the hallway where Austin waved out from the automatic doors. I waved back as he sprinted off down the road.

I paced the hall outside Tristan's room and heard what sounded like fighting.

"Tristan!" I banged on the door.

"Hang on a second," he yelled out.

The door opened and Tristan was wrapped in a towel. "Who were you yelling at?" I asked as I looked around the room.

There was a pink bra tossed over a chair and I realized Tristan was still dirty, his towel wasn't wet, but beads of sweat were dripping down his forehead.

"You can come out, Alexa," I said as I crossed my arms.

"Sorry, I told him to be quiet," Alexa emerged from the bathroom in a small towel that barely covered her.

"If your parents find out you guys are screwing...that's a far cry more than having a little crush on each other," I felt my stomach turn at the impossible rage they'd face from Arthur.

"We haven't..." Tristan rushed to say.

"We were about to... we never get to be alone, Carrie," Alexa begged.

"Look, I wasn't here... keep it down and please use protection!" I winked, as I left the room Alexa sprung from her towel and into Tristan's arms and it brought warmth to me to see how they had grown over the years. I couldn't help but smirk a little as I closed to door behind me. There was something about being that young and in lust, it was all around me right now.

"Is Alexa in there?" Mindy asked as she stormed through the hallway.

"Umm, I'm not sure. I was just collecting my thoughts. I just had a run-in with Ezra," I lied, and my hands began to shake.

"Move, Carrie!" Mindy ordered as she saw right through my lie.

Mindy bashed her fists on the door. We all knew when Mindy had a feeling about something, she was usually right, and she was about to put a hole in the door.

"Open the goddamn door, Tristan or I will burn it down!" She yelled.

Lucy and Celinde came out to see what all the commotion was. Tristan opened the door flustered and bright red.

"Mother!" Alexa whined from within the room.

I couldn't see her; Mindy shoved past Tristan and collected the bra from the chair. I moved back toward Lucy and motioned for her to go back into the room.

"How long have you two been at this?" Mindy screamed.

"This was the first time…" Tristan bravely re-entered the room in a desperate plea to protect Alexa.

"Arthur told you both that this wasn't going to happen," she sighed.

"Well, aren't you the perfect hypocrite; so, it's okay for you and dad to sneak around the Precinct and the bunker but not us?" Alexa argued.

"That's different! We are married, Tristan is only barely hanging onto his humanity by a thread," she growled.

"I am the thread MOTHER! Me! he hangs on, for me!" Alexa cried.

Her heart sank as Tristan dropped into the chair and held his face in his hands as tears began to flood his eyes.

Alexa rushed to him and held his face in her hands. They were so in love, and they had been for months, if not years; from the time Tristan guarded her against the horror around us the moment Kyle took his last breath. Tristan was arguably the most dangerous of them, but her innocence was calming and tamed his wild nature. She weakened him and he shared his strength with her in return.

"Mindy…" I called out.

She looked over to me as Alexa sat naked, exposed, and fearless of the world she grew into.

"What have we become," Mindy sobbed.

I caught her as she fell, and I pulled her from the room to the chair in the corridor.

"What did I do wrong?" she wept.

"You didn't do anything wrong; she can't help who she loves," I nodded.

I could feel Celinde and Lucy spying on me from their doorway. We were a hotel full of women on emotional highs and lows.

"I don't want this life for her, Carrie," Mindy slapped my shoulders and shook my body in her rage.

"It's not your choice anymore, Mindy. She's a woman now," I said in Alexa's defense.

Mindy's eyes rose and locked with mine and I feared she might strike me. Mindy was bigger than I was and had a temper that could rival Graham's.

She sunk to the ground and held my legs drenching my jeans in snot and tears as the rest of us stood frozen in terror.

Alexa emerged from the room dressed and she descended to Mindy's level and hugged her before me.

"I'm okay, he treats me well, he'd never hurt me," Alexa whispered.

Tristan stood in the doorway with sad eyes knowing his relationship with Alexa would never be accepted.
"I want you to leave this place, go far away from here, and live a full life Alexa, go to college, have a family," Mindy squeezed her tightly.

"This is the only life I know, it's the only one I want..." Alexa confessed.

Tristan closed the door and walked quietly down the hall with tears in his eyes. Ezra met him at the end of the hallway and took him outside to sit in the carpark.

"I'll never approve of him, Alexa," Mindy sighed.

"Then I'll just have to live with that, I need him more than I need your approval," Alexa stood up and raced down the hall to the carpark.

The tension from that point on was high, Mindy kept close to Izzy who also shared her feelings about the young relationship, but Tristan and Alexa were inseparable once again.

V.J.Garland

Chapter Five

Jax

Graham was faster, but I was bigger. I hurled him further down the halls, Christian beside me and Arthur now hauling Clarence into walls, but he was quicker to submit.

"Lock them in the infirmary!" I shouted.

"That won't hold…" Jake gasped.

I ignored him, even though what he said was true, that door wasn't even strong enough to hold the chickens for a week, it was useless. But I couldn't have them wandering, not for a while. The girls needed time to get as far away as possible.

Liam and Austin would've caught up with them by now and they'd be able to talk Carrie and Celinde down. Arthur was an agitated mess. Mindy *and* Alexa left when I ordered them all away. This had been discussed between me, Ezra, and Arthur on multiple occasions. We just didn't think it would happen so soon; or that Celinde of all people might trigger it.

"Are you alright?" I asked Christian.
"I just don't know how I got here— like this?" he sighed.

"It was bound to happen; it wasn't just us locked away in cabins. They were confined to this steel box; it was eating away at them," I replied.

"Celinde wanted more, she wanted normal, how could I ever give her that? I couldn't even fuck her without almost tearing her a new orifice. She just always thought it would get better," Christian groaned.

"Do you feel better?" I asked.

"I feel lost…even more so now she's gone," he admitted.

"Who broke it off?" I asked.

"I did, I wanted her to get out of here and get her life back," he said.

"And then she lost it…" I sighed.

"I guess for the last few years all she's lived for is us, for me? she doesn't even know how things are back home? we've been in this protective bubble for so long," he blurted.

He was right, nobody checked on the outside world past Kamloops, and Izzy and Mindy only went out every few months for supplies not out to coffee with gossipy girlfriends. Nobody had phones, the only TVs we had only played old DVDs, and the internet was non-existent.

We didn't even have a functional radio. We never needed that stuff—we were living almost completely off the grid out here.

"Hopefully they find some purpose without us all holding them back," I added.

"What about Ezra, Tristan, Liam, and Austin? Are they coming back?" he asked.

"Everyone is free to make their own decisions over the next twenty-four hours, except those idiots in there," I announced to the others.

We barricaded the bunker doors from the outside and headed back down the soggy pathway that led to the center of Wolftown. Affectionately named by Alexa in her younger years when she was allowed to come down to learn to hunt with Tristan and Austin. Most of the cabins were clustered together. Mine was further away from the center, I mapped everything out the night Kyle lost it. Away was safer for me, and anyone wandering near my cabin was doing so for a reason. There were the odd random cabins that were used for newcomers who needed confinement, they were heavily dressed in chains and reinforced and terrifying to look at from a human eye. They were spaced on the outskirts and rarely used.

Christian called a meeting in the town center — I cringed inside.

Power came with consequences; Carrie always held the responsibility. We had run a convincing façade for far too long and now I had to show my face and follow it up with a werewolf's anonymous meeting with wolves who were about to find out their den mothers had been forced to abandon ship. Dread consumed me and then Arthur dragged me up onto an empty keg and told the others to shut up and listen—I wanted to vomit.

Questions racked my *own* brain as I glared out at gloomy frustrated faces. Where do I even begin?

"Where's Clarence?" One asked.

"He's chained up with Graham," I answered.

"Why?" Another asked.

"Graham was attacking the humans, you all know they feed us, and supply us with the things we need to feel human, all of them were friends to us," I expressed.

"That's why they lived a life of luxury? While we suffered with leaky roofs and moldy bread!" Evan scowled as he appeared from the back of the crowd.

"Nobody said you had to stay here, Evan. You're welcome to leave at any time," I sneered.

"I think a lot of us would like you and your pack to leave…" Arthur grumbled aloud as he supported my remark.

A loud thud clambered through the valley and down below we could see the bunker doors crash into the ground as Graham and Clarence exploded out of the hole.

They sprung down the hill on all fours, claws long, sharpened, and with one objective in mind— me.

Graham was impressive, his transformations were buttery, not drawn out like most of us. This was his advantage; he would skulk around Wolftown and convince the others he'd show them how if they supported his claim to power. The Precinct had become a democracy. Even as a werewolf, I couldn't escape politics.

There was muttering, bickering, and soon shoving, then punching and brawls broke out.
Christian raced to break them up, but I held him back.

"They'll stop, just let them unleash their anger," I ordered.

"They'll be back at it again when they realize, we have no one here keeping us fed, keeping us human," Otis muttered.

"No humans?" One heard over the fighting.

"Be careful, Jax. You're slipping," Evan warned with a grin.

Graham chuckled beside him as blood spatter flung through the crowd of unhappy werewolves.

"STOP THIS!" I growled.

My hands broke first, then my hair thick and barbed pressed its way out of my skin as my bones could be heard breaking. Everyone stopped and watched as my muzzle stretched and my fangs were barred, and my height grew as well as my width.
Most bowed down once they knew my size was no match for their own. Stories always spread through the village about me. The cannibal, the one who drenched a whole beach in blood and consumed every wolf who challenged

me. It was mostly true, but I had no desire to be that again.

I felt my eyes burning as they matched the hue of the super-blood moon that reflected a red stain onto the river behind Wolftown.

"His eyes…" I heard one man whisper.

My eyes were once yellow, a good sign. It mostly meant that the werewolf lived a harmonious life, orange was a little more alarming, they had a mixed diet, same as the silvers they were edgier, it was better to be on high alert around them, but red was bad, red seemed to have no way of turning back. I'd lived a vegetarian lifestyle since Cannon Beach, but my eyes were like a gruesome brand. So, I made sure nobody here ever saw me as a wolf — until now.

Carrie had helped me keep that secret, maybe she was the one who spread the rumors to keep everyone else in line. Or maybe she didn't, I didn't know the origin of it all, just the whispers I heard through hollow walls miles down the muddy road from my cabin.

The whispering stopped once I let out a deep roar that shook the ground beneath me. Graham and his pose jumped back somewhat.

Christian stood in my place and spoke out explaining the situation with the girls and what that meant for our supply chain. He was thorough and answered most questions with ease and did what he could to bring harmony back to the Precinct while I wandered through the crowd and intimidated those who I knew were breeding trouble and doubt. They got an extra snarl and stream of dribble over the shoulder. I wasn't opposed to scare tactics.

I slowly morphed back to my human form— I had made my point.

"Are they coming back?" Evan snickered cheekily.

"Soon..." I answered.

"As you were..." I ordered as I stepped away from the circle wrapping around me.

Everyone stepped away and I sighed a breath of relief as we managed to diffuse a potentially devasting situation.

"Jamal, you and Otis go up to the bunker and see what supplies we have left," I ordered.

"Christian, you and Jake go check the fields Austin was planting last summer," they nodded and walked off.

"Arthur, you and I better go hunting," I sighed.

"What about me?" Henry asked.

"I need you to keep an eye on things around here, this could flare up again at any minute," I grunted.
"We'll come hunting, you'll need a lot more than the two of you can carry," said Reggie as he walked over with Jensen and the others in his close circle.

"I'd appreciate your help," I nodded as I shook his hand.

"Fred and Serg, you guys stay and help Henry," Reggie said to the younger of his friends.

Reggie and his crew grew over time, he had a knack for making friends easily and he was trustworthy.

"Good luck," Henry grabbed my hand and slapped me on the back with his other and had a genuine look of fear in his eyes.

"We'll be as quick as we can, just don't be picky with what we bring back," I laughed.

Jamal and Otis were pushing wheelbarrows down the path as we were heading out full of Goldfish crackers, stale bread, and old blocks of cheese.

"I hope nobody's lactose intolerant," Arthur chuckled.

"It'll work for now," I saluted them as we transformed and leaped off down the dirt roads on our way to the better-known hunting tracks that Tristan had told us about.

CHAPTER SIX

LUCY

Things seemed to calm down between Mindy and Alexa enough for the rest of us to get some sleep. Ezra, Liam, and Austin dropped sandwiches at everyone's doors while Carrie did her best to pretend that she was asleep. Celinde was in the shower.

It was 10 am when I woke the next day; it didn't even feel like I had blinked, I was still wired. I walked down the hallway to the vending machine and squeezed past housekeeping and sneakily stole some extra shampoo and conditioner. Those one-use tiny bottles didn't stretch far for three of us girls in one room. Celinde had butt-length mousey brown hair now that her salon blonde had grown out, she alone needed two of each.

"Ah, miss! You need to ask for those," the housekeeper had sprung me.

"Sorry, there's a few of us in our room, one wasn't enough," I apologized.

"That's okay, but you only need to ask. Do you need more towels?" She asked kindly.

"That would be wonderful if you could bring some in," I smiled still embarrassed.

"What's your room number?" she asked.

"Eleven," I replied.

"I'll be there soon," she smiled back.

I hung my head in shame as I walked back to the room, closed the door behind me, and took in a deep breath.

"What now?" Celinde grunted and yawned. She was back to being grumpy.

"Ahh, it's nothing. Housekeeping is bringing up some more towels," I smiled.

"Brilliant, I might actually get to shower with a dry towel," Carrie cast a glower at Celinde who had used all the towels last night.

A loud knock pounded on the door, and I went to open it.

"Oh, Mindy! Good morning," I smiled.

"Not who you were expecting?" she mused.

"No, I was expecting shampoo and towels, but you'll suffice," I laughed.

"I'd kill for a day with a hairdresser…" Mindy sighed as she moved into the room.

"How's Alexa?" Carrie asked.

"Still giving me the cold shoulder. Tristan on the other hand won't leave me alone. That's why I'm hiding in here," she admitted.

"Izzy?" I asked.

"She's been on the john all night, the sandwich Austin gave her was off I think, she's sleeping it off now," Mindy winced.

"Oh, dear…" Celinde gulped.

"Where are the guys?" Carrie asked curiously.

"Asleep on the floor of our room," Mindy sighed.

"I should talk to Ezra…" Carrie grumbled.

Carrie had been quiet all night, I could see thoughts quizzing her mind as she stared at the ceiling whilst she lay on the floor so Celinde and I could get a decent night's sleep.

There was a gentle knock at the door and this time I knew it was my towels.

"Come in," I said cheerfully as I opened the door.

The housekeeper came in backward with her trolley and handed me a pile of fresh warm towels, a caddy of body wash, shampoo, conditioner, and a brown bag of packaged muffins, sandwiches, and some pieces of fresh fruit.

"You are so sweet! Thank you so much," I expressed as I unexpectedly hugged her.

"Oh! You're welcome," she hugged me back.

"Is that you Kitty Flores," Mindy was in her face examining her closely.

"Oh my, I never thought I'd see you again, Mindy…" Kitty scowled.

"Well, I'll be damned!" Celinde gasped.

"I've got a good mind to take all of that back," she hissed.

"Oh no, please don't," I grumbled and held the items closer to me.

"What are you doing here?" Carrie asked.

"It took me days to find my way back here, I was broke. So, I came back here begging for help. The manager offered me a job, but the pay is so shit I can only afford to keep a room and buy food," she glowered.

"Still got that sass I see," Mindy smiled.

"Forget whatever you heard Mindy, it's irrelevant now," Carrie interrupted.

"How do I get back there?" Kitty asked.

"You want to go back there?" Carrie was curious.

"I didn't end things well with Jake," she sighed.

"As if you even care…" Mindy laughed.

"Of course, I care! He's, my husband. See, I still wear my wedding ring!" She held out her hand and Mindy gave a reluctant smile.

"Yes, I kissed Jamal, but I never slept with him, and that kiss was a mistake. I was feeling trapped in a new marriage trying to navigate a new way of living. I was a wild child and I strayed from Jake, and I regret it every day," she cried.

"I'm sorry, Kitty," Mindy hugged her apologetically.

"Can you take me to see him?" she said as she wiped away her tears.

"We aren't going back to the Precinct," Carrie snapped unexpectedly.

"You guys saw what was happening when we left, it's bigger than Jax now, there could be fighting and killing, we aren't safe there anymore…" she sighed.

"I don't care, I'll go on my own just draw me a map!" Kitty begged.

"I'll go with you…" I stepped forward.

"No, Lucy!" Celinde argued. She'd warmed to me just in time to object and think it would count.

"I have to know he's okay," I shook my head.

"I'll come too," Alexa said from the doorway.

"Oh, definitely not!" Mindy yelled.

"My father is still there! I'll never know peace if I don't, how can you just walk away from him?" Alexa growled.

"When this all happened, we made a deal. If it got too dangerous, I would take you away. That's what I did," she sighed.

"I'm not a little girl anymore, mama," Alexa announced as she looked to Carrie and Celinde for support.

"I'll take them, I promise I'll look after them…" Tristan sprung up from behind Alexa.

His eyes locked with Carrie's, and she nodded permitting him. Celinde slumped back onto the bed and let out a deep breath.

"You've got two days, get in and out as quickly as you can. If you aren't back, we're leaving without you," Celinde shouted from the pillows.

"Leaving to go where?" Kitty asked.

"Home!" Celinde responded.

"Home? Home doesn't exist anymore…" she sighed.

"What do you mean?" Carrie questioned.

"You don't know?" Kitty sighed.

"Know what?" Celinde sat up to attention.

"Astoria has been wiped out, most of Oregon and Washington are uninhabitable, and it's spreading down to California now," she began.

"What is spreading, Kitty?" Carrie got in her face and grabbed her shoulders.

"The werewolves…They keep turning people, they aren't just killing them anymore," She grabbed Carrie's wrist and pulled them off her.

"When did this start happening?" Celinde asked.

"A few days ago. I hadn't heard anything about werewolves until then, now they are all over the news. There's footage everywhere. Seattle is currently being evacuated," She grabbed the TV remote and switched on the news.

We all sat at the end of the bed and watched chaos and fear take over the TV. It was like a movie, but it wasn't. People were jumping out of buildings only to be caught at the bottom in the clutches of a wolf's jaw.

"This could wipe out the whole country..." Tristan sighed as he held Alexa in his arms.

Tristan seemed to struggle with his identity more than the others, he had my pity.

Mindy watched them and observed his tender touches, I felt a warmth leave her body as if she would finally submit to them.

"Here, go now!" Mindy handed Tristan the keys to the Jeep.

"Tell Jax what's happening. Lucy, he'll listen to you," She hugged me as only a mother could.

"I will," I nodded.

"Be safe," Carrie hugged me next followed by Celinde.

"Tell Christian I understand...please," she brushed my hair off my face and held my cheek.

I nodded and hugged her back and just as quickly was pulled away by Kitty. Mindy threw her some clothes of Carrie's as she rushed out of the door in her maid's uniform.

Izzy passed us in the hallway, she was green and looking exceptionally unwell.

"Is that you Kitty Flores?" Izzy stopped us.

"Mindy and the others will explain," Kitty smiled.

"You don't look well, get some rest," Alexa hugged her goodbye.

We finally got to the carpark and climbed into the jeep. Tristan drove and we set off back to the Precinct. Alexa sat in the front and Kitty and me in the back.

"I've got some catching up to do. How do you know these guys?" Kitty asked me.

"Long story short, my car broke down and I walked a million miles through Willmore till I came across Jax's cabin," I explained.

"And you guys hit it off?" She pressed.

"I like him, I find him attractive, and I don't want bad things to happen to him," I laughed at her curiousness.

"I see," she smiled.

"How's Jake," She tapped Tristan on the shoulder.

"Ah, good as can be. We live in the same cabin, he's a good man," Tristan answered.

"Does he ever talk about me?" she asked.

"Some days, it was hard for him to make you leave. But after what happened with Kyle, he knew he was doing the right thing," he answered.

"That was fucked up…" Kitty sighed.

"Who's Kyle?" I asked.

"He was Jax's best friend," Alexa replied.

"What happened to him?" I asked.

Everyone was quiet, nobody wanted to answer me, and I pressed a little harder.

"Come on!" I snapped.

"Kyle was going to kill Jax. Jax is the big dog. If he dies, that takes the rest of us out. Jax killed him instead," Tristan explained.

"But that would kill him too?" I asked.

"Kyle was human..." Kitty sighed.

"Ohhh..." I realized the gravity of the situation now.

"He wasn't okay, Lucy. Kyle was one tantrum away from a full-fledged mental breakdown," Alexa added.

"He was falling pretty hard for Carrie, but she had just met Ezra and they were becoming a thing," Kitty explained.

"And that's why she worked so hard to ensure Jax remained in power and protected," Tristan said.

"Wish she had worked that hard to maintain the bunker..." Alexa groaned.

"What happened in the bunker?" Tristan asked.

"The last two winters we had too many newcomers, she was giving them our rations. She said it was better to keep them fed or they'd make a meal of us...so we ate only every few days," Alexa said as she held back tears.

"I had no idea… Why didn't she tell me? I would have gone and hunted more," Tristan sighed.

"She said she noticed the kills were getting smaller, and there were not as many as when we first built the Precinct. The animals were fleeing the area, she didn't want you wandering off too far," Alexa explained.

"Stupid woman," Kitty snarled.

"She was trying…" Alexa snapped.

"By starving you all…I don't think that's a solution," Kitty argued.

"It was survival, it wasn't a long-term fix, Kitty," Alexa growled back.

"Well, I'm glad I wasn't around for that," Kitty shrugged.

"No, you were just working for minimum wage and living in a shoe box, eating takeout, and watching Netflix," Tristan teased.

"Okay, let's not do this…" I interrupted.

"Do what?" Tristan laughed.

"We are going to a very dangerous place, we don't need to alienate one another," I scowled.

"You're right. Sorry, Lucy," Alexa sighed.

"That's why Jax likes you, you're sensible," Tristan smiled.

"I wouldn't call stealing off of my trolley sensible," Kitty laughed.

"And I still didn't get to wash my hair after all of that," I laughed with her.

The ride was silent for the next half of the way. Snow was coming down heavily and the road was becoming harder to see.

Tristan decided to pull the Jeep over while the storm passed.

"There are blankets in the back," Alexa pointed.

"Wanna snuggle up and keep warm," Kitty chuckled as she shared a blanket between us that felt itchy and old.

"I won't say no," I laughed, and we huddled together.

V.J.Garland

CHAPTER SEVEN

GRAHAM

Jax had raced off with several others around the back out of sight from most of the others, the rest of his following kept up appearances by hauling food in from the bunker and fields.

"We should follow him," Evan snarled.

"I've got a better idea," I raced to an unknown path that gave us a shorter more direct road to Kamloops, that's where Mindy and Izzy usually went to stock up on supplies. They'd have to be there.

"Come on!" I yelled out.

Max followed first, he was tall, skinny, and offensive in his manner, the kind of guy you kept away from your girlfriend. He wasn't a part of our group, but he seemed agitated when Jax was prowling around slobbering on my guys. He was disposable for what I needed so I let him come along. Luis also followed, he had no business being a werewolf, he was short, stumpy, and lazy and only had the energy to walk when he was in his wolf form which he seemed to inhibit far more than what was appropriate down in the Precinct.

Granted they were the outsiders, but more bodies would help me make my stand. Jax had built a decent little home here, better than anything I'd seen in my century as a werewolf.

We wouldn't outnumber them, but it would be an even fight. If he wanted to avoid it, all he had to do was put me in charge and go away quietly.

A snowstorm was coming in, it was getting too heavy to walk as humans.

"Wolf out, everyone!" I ordered.

It took me seconds to change, far longer for the others. The night was overhead and I zoned in on the main road a mile ahead, I could hear breathing, but no cars running.

The others smelt it too and we raced towards the hotbox of humans. It'd been months since I'd tasted a human.

I raised my claws and signaled to pause.

Tristan, I could smell his scent and hear his snoring. He wasn't alone, but he was the only wolf in the area.

We crept forward until we reached the road, Luis looked like a fat Yeti, the snow had clung to his oily fur and made him even fluffier than before.

I pounced onto the bonnet of the Jeep and Tristan woke, stunned by the loud thud and me staring back at him. He had pretty little Alexa sitting beside him and two girls in the back, one I didn't recognize.

"What do you want Graham," Tristan yelled through the window.

"Where's Carrie," I've got some stuff to add to the shopping list, I chuckled as I morphed back.

"She's not here," Tristan growled as he stepped out of the car and into the storm.

"Tristan!" Alexa called, but he slammed the door before she could finish.

"Don't hurt them..." his voice was shaky as he almost pleaded with me.

"Tell me where Carrie is, and I'll leave you alone to freeze to death... is that the kinder option you want? or should we just get it over with? I'll make it quick," I smiled.

"Tell me Graham, have you always been an asshole, or has being a werewolf for so long weighed out any empathy you had left," Tristan asked.

"Nah, I've always been an asshole, I just get to be more of an asshole now," I winked.

"They're about an hour from here..." Tristan began to say.

"NO, Tristan!" Alexa screamed as she jumped out of the car.

"Just because you were raised by werewolves doesn't make you one of us, listen to your boyfriend before I make a snack out of you!" Evan grimaced as he pressed her between his body and the Jeep.

Evan always had a thing for Alexa, she was strong-spirited, and he made it no secret he loved a young challenging woman.

"Take her," I ordered.

Clarence and Luis held Tristan down as Evan tore away at Alexa's clothes exposing her to the elements.

"Get it over with!" I yelled to Evan.

Alexa did her best to fight back but she was no match for two men twice her size, definitely not in their wolf forms.

Tristan morphed but he was smaller than the rest of us, he was faster but no match for strength. He growled loudly and his howls shook the snow burying the car with the other two girls inside. Screams echoed through the valley they were parked in, Tristan took his best shot and bit into Luis's neck, he broke free for a moment as Evan attempted to mount Alexa. He thrashed his claws across the back of Evan's neck, he dropped to the ground releasing Alexa.

"Tristan!" The other girls screamed.

Clarence began digging in the snow as I fought Tristan back. He was stronger than I gave him credit for, but I was landing bigger hits and it wasn't long before he blacked out.

Alexa that sneaky little bitch had a hunting knife and was stabbing Evan repeatedly.

"Get away from him!" She screamed as I hovered over Tristan's bloodied body.

She was shaking, mostly out of fear, I could feel her adrenaline pumping, and the heat radiated from her body as she threatened to slice Evan's neck wide open.

"You know we'll find her, Alexa. Tell me where she is and I'll let you and your boyfriend live just one more day," I offered as I retracted my claws and took a step closer to her while Clarence dragged the girls from the snow-filled car.

"I'm right here," Carrie tapped me on the shoulder and smiled.

"CARRIE!" Alexa raced to hug her.

"Good, now we can talk business," I nodded.

"I don't do business with the likes of you, Graham. You are banished from the Precinct, if you ever try to come back, I'll kill you myself, and your dogs," she looked around at the others, Evan was healing and trying to sit up.

"Big words my fiery friend, pity you're a human, you'd make one hell of a werewolf," I teased.

"Leave…last chance," she winked.

"I'm not Jax, I don't take orders from humans," I bared my teeth and growled.

CHAPTER EIGHT

JAX

"What was that?" I asked Arthur.

"Probably just the water coming from the falls over there," he replied.

We raced closer to the falls but there was no water running, it was completely iced over.

"There's a road up there, I heard people!" I pressed.

We all raced up the hill and the voices got louder.

"It's Alexa!" Arthur forced out his werewolf and launched himself down a powder-filled road, I was feet behind him, the others not so far off.

We hung back a moment, Liam, Austin, and Ezra have perched up above on another hill ready to pounce.

It was Carrie, Alexa, Kitty, Lucy, and Tristan. Graham had found them. The others were nowhere to be seen.

Graham threw Carrie to the ground, but she was staunch and didn't make a sound. Alexa cried for help as Evan restrained her from trying to wake Tristan.

"Tristan!" She screamed over and over.

Ezra dropped from the hill on top of Graham, tearing him away from Carrie, Austin dove in next, pushing Evan away from Alexa and Liam stood in front of the rest of their group.

Arthur raced over and picked up Tristan and whisked him off back down the hill toward the frozen waterfall.

"You just can't stay out of trouble," I said as I approached Graham.

"You came out of your cabin, twice in one day, you ill?" he joked.

I snickered back and Ezra threw him into the ground. I kicked him across the face and snapped one of his fangs in half.

"Argh!" Graham groaned.

"Kill him!" Lucy begged.

"You've got a lot to learn, girl!" Evan laughed.

"What does that mean?" Lucy asked.

"We stopped killing our kind a long time ago," I sighed.

"But you killed your best friend! KILL HIM JAX or he's going to come after you next!" Kitty screamed.

"Werewolves are hard to kill…" I sighed.

"Don't ever come back here, or I'll do worse than kill you," I punched the other side of his muzzle and he fell into the snow.

Lucy raced to my side, and I held her securely in my arms as we walked to catch up with Arthur and Tristan.

"Why did you let him go…" Lucy asked.

"I don't have what I need to permanently put him down right now without jeopardizing myself, but we outnumber them here. If he follows us back there's enough colloidal to take him out still in the Wolftown well," I explained.

"The well?" Carrie asked.

"I had to retain some power and secrets," I smiled.

"You filled the well with colloidal?" she laughed.

"To be honest Care, you were so business all this time, I was worried your hold would become too much…" I started.

"And I'd become as powerful over you as Wesley was to Tristan and their pack," she pieced it together.

"Exactly," I sighed.

We walked together and got half a mile from the waterfall, then I heard the anger brewing behind me. Evan was racing down towards us with Luis and Clarence, Graham, and Max walking slower behind them.

Evan lunged for Ezra; he wasn't playing anymore. He was tearing chunks from him, and every bite stopped Ezra's transformation from taking hold.

I chased after Graham while Liam tore Evan from Ezra. Alexa, Kitty, and Lucy formed a circle back-to-back. Alexa holding the hunting knife that Tristan had given her, and Lucy had Liam's old tomahawk axe he kept stashed in the Jeep.

Graham tore me to the ground, and we were like a ball of tumbleweed snapping and clawing at one another, we fell down the waterfall and barely broke the ice as we skidded back and forth over the wet slippery surface.

Liam and Luis fell next. Their impact shattered one corner of the river as they fell into the freezing cold water and desperately tried to climb out.

Carrie was on Ezra's back; they tumble down together with Max right behind them. They tried to fight him off together, but he had a serious height advantage.

Alexa was small and tried to climb down on an icicle, and Lucy was on another as they used their weapons to chip small edges for grip, but it was too slippery.

Kitty jumped down into the water and Evan snapped her in his grip as she tumbled down. Lucy dropped down, swam through the icy blades to Kitty's aid, and thrashed the axe into Evan's chest. It barely made any impact, Alexa appeared behind him and forced her knife into his back, he fell forward, and Kitty pulled out the axe.

"Strike for the arm!" Alexa ordered.

Reggie and Jensen held him taught as they lunged into every hit.

Tristan and Arthur raced through still dizzied but eager to help. Arthur went for Luis and Tristan for Max.

Alexa and Kitty had successfully cut off Evan's arm. Once it was off, he passed out; they tried to lift it, but they weren't strong enough. I raced in and took the arm and used it to slash a hole in Graham's chest.

"That won't kill you, but it'll put you down long enough for me to make an example out of you," I sighed.

"Pick them up. We're bringing them back," I ordered.

The girls were tired, and half frozen by the time we made it back to the Precinct.

Lucy walked away from the crowds of people and werewolves alike and took solace in my cabin, Kitty followed. It was quieter there, a good distance away from Wolftown.

"Alexa, go with them, you don't need to see this," Carrie ordered.

"You too, Carrie," I urged.

"What?" she objected.

"This is werewolf business, you don't need to see this," I sighed.

Ezra nodded as he agreed with me and walked her off to the cabin.

I hauled Graham behind me into Wolftown and slammed his body down as hard as I could into the stone podium.

His bones could be heard breaking as he screamed out in pain.

"What the fuck happened?" Christian asked bewildered as he looked us all over.

Ezra was by far the worst with flesh missing from his shoulder and neck, but he was still standing and his wounds slowly healed before us.

"We gave them a chance to leave, they wanted to fight," I explained.

"Where's Celinde?" Christian gasped.

"We didn't see them," I sighed.

"She's safe, she's at Kamloops," Liam replied.

"Jake…" Carrie had snuck out of the cabin.

"Carrie!" I growled.

"I know, but Kitty's here…" she explained.

"Take me to her!" Jake raced off with Carrie.

I paced the center of the meeting point and looked between the well and scum that took up space and resources.

"There'll be a public execution in 20mins!" I called out.

Many looked over and whispers started once again. Jamal and Henry came down with Otis and some others followed by Fred and Serg.

"Are you sure about this?" Christian asked.

"I tried to let them go, we walked away, but they came after us," I explained.

"Okay, well let's do this," Christian agreed.

"Let's fill it up!" I nodded as Christian, and Liam brought out barrel after barrel of fresh colloidal silver to hurl into the well.

"I'm not touching that shit…" Christian stepped back.

"I'll do it," Tristan offered.

He and I were the only ones here who had ever felt the burn and he'd felt it on a completely different level than what I had.

"You're sure? I could get Carrie," Ezra interjected.

"Carrie needs to collect herself before she ends up like my father," Tristan obliged.

I locked eyes with him and nodded in agreeance as I popped the lids on the barrels, we poured them together down the well carefully.

Headlights beamed down the road that led to the bunker, but they were flashing brighter than normal and then there was loud honking.

The car didn't stop, it pummeled down the uneven path and came to a sudden stop just outside of the first cabins.

Izzy, Mindy, and Celinde leaped from the run-down old vehicle and raced toward me.

"We've got a problem," Celinde said.

"I know, we're taking care of it now," I pointed to Graham and his unconscious comrades.

"Not them… we need them, something's happened and if all he wants is power and a healthy diet, give it to him, Jax!" Celinde pleaded.

"What are you talking about?" Christian intervened.

"Seattle is under attack," she cried.

"Attack from what?" we asked at the same time.

"Werewolves, this isn't a secret anymore," Mindy added.

Izzy slapped Graham's face until he woke up.

"Graham, you piece of shit!" she yelled in his face.

"What did I do now?" he sighed between his grumbles of pain.

"How is a whole city being evacuated because of a werewolf pandemic after all these years?" she asked.

"How would I know?" he laughed.

"You're the oldest one here…"

"No, Clarence is…" he huffed.

"CLARENCE!" I yelled and kicked him awake.

"You can't stop it, Jax," he smiled through a bloodied mouth.

"Does anyone know ANYTHING about this?" Christian barked with worry.

"It's the Olivet solar eclipse," Clarence coughed through sputum.

"What is that?" Ezra asked.

"A once in one-hundred-year occurrence… it just so happens to rebirth every dead werewolf for the whole moon phase, then they're dust again," he continued.

"That's not good news," My jaw dropped slightly.

"Are you telling the truth?" Christian gripped him by the neck.

"Look around you, Christian. Look to the sky— what do you see?" he asked.

The crowd looked above, the sky was clear for a winter's night, but the air just above us was foggy, and birds flew about agitated and restless beneath a beaming red moon that stained the river red.

"I have nothing to gain from lying to you," Clarence sat upright as he wiped off his face.

"Every wolf?" I asked.

"EVERY wolf…" he nodded.

"You've seen this happen before?" graham enquired.

"Just once, but there wasn't enough of us to cause something so bad that the powers that be couldn't cover up," he replied.

"But in the last hundred years, that might've changed," I gasped.

"We need to get home…" Christian grabbed my arm.

"And do what?" Tristan argued.

"Anyone who was alive isn't anymore," Graham added.

I raced back to my cabin and flung the door open.

The girls were sitting around the fireplace, sipping coffee and tea out of mugs, glasses, and bowls.

"How'd it go?" Carrie asked.

"It didn't, not yet. Something's happened and I need to know if it's true before I do it," I sighed.

"Whatever it is, don't trust them!" She snapped back.

Mindy and Izzy were behind me catching their breath in the doorway.

"What was on the news?" I asked.

"Werewolves, everywhere, they were wreaking havoc on towns and cities," Mindy explained.

"You're sure it wasn't a movie though?" Lucy asked still miffed at the idea.

"It was definitely not a movie, you were there," Kitty mumbled.

"Why isn't it happening here?" Jake asked.

"It's happening all through South America, it seems the only parts of North America being affected so far are Washington, Oregon, and California and it's spilling into Idaho," Kitty added.

"It won't be far away then…" I sighed.

"We should try to contain it," Carrie grumbled.

"You need to stay put. We'll go, I can't keep putting you in harm's way," I replied.

"Fuck that! I'm coming," she argued.

"I need someone here, someone who's respected and that the others will listen to," I pressed.

"That should be you!" She growled.

"If I can see Joel again, Carrie," I began.

"He died a werewolf, I have a chance to see him again," I wiped a tear from my eye before it trickled down my cheek.

"So, you'll go home?" She asked.

"I'll try if I don't come back…"

"Don't even finish that sentence," Lucy leaped to hug me.

"You're coming back," she wept.

I held her as close as I could without hurting her and felt her body heaving through her cries.

"It'll be okay…" I said as I stroked her back.

The others jumped up and left the cabin to give us some space. I could hear Jake making arrangements with Tristan as he approached the cabin, but all I could focus on was Lucy.

"I just got you back," she held my face in her hands.

"I will come back for you, this isn't goodbye, we've barely just got this started," I smiled and kissed her forehead.

"Why do you have to go," she said as tears streamed down her face.

"If I can see my little brother just one more time, I'll cherish that forever, but all I have right now is a memory of a pie-faced down on the floor and his screams haunting me every waking moment," I explained.

"What about the ones who killed him?" She asked.

"That's why we're all going..." I replied.

"Wait, all of you?" she gasped.

"Graham, Evan, Clarence?" she inquired.

"You are all safer if we clear out the Precinct. I don't know what this moon phase means for us, you shouldn't be surrounded by a pack of werewolves," I pressed.

"EVERYONE?" Christian slammed the door open.

Lucy peeled herself away from me as I turned to face Christian.

"It makes sense, but that's a lot of werewolves," he said.

"It's an army..." I added.

"We might need one if we come across those guys who killed Noah," Christian sighed.

"And my brothers?" Tristan sighed.

"Tristan..." I began.

"It's okay, I'm just relieved my dad won't be coming back," he nodded.

Alexa hugged him from behind and peaked her head around his ribs.

"Let's get organized and break the news…" Jake suggested.

"Come on," I said as I offered my hand to Lucy to walk with me down to Wolftown.

She grasped my hand and followed, Kitty beside her and Jake not far behind her.

"When this is all over, we'll rebuild," I squeezed her hand.

"If you want to stay of course," I added quickly.

She looked at me curiously and held my gaze a little longer and she fumbled with my fingers.

"Rebuild?" she whispered.

"I might need to negotiate with Graham and Clarence," I sighed.

"You would give up the Precinct?" Jake interrupted.

"That darn werewolf hearing…" I muttered.

"Maybe, we'll see what happens," I added.

Jake was uneasy about the idea as we walked towards the town center.

Christian began spreading the word of a meeting and soon we were all gathered once more.

"We're all here because we wanted to live a harmonious life. A life where our families wouldn't have to fear us, where we could live together in a safe place. There seems to be a new threat with the looming moon phase. Something that happens only once in one hundred years," I began.

"What does that mean?" asked Olivia, Jensen's girlfriend," She had come down with some of the other partners who took cover in the back end of the bunker.

"It means every werewolf who ever lived, gets to come back till the moon finishes a full cycle," Graham said.

"A full cycle?" Kitty enquired.

"A complete rotation," I added.

"So, a month?" Olivia confirmed.

"Yes," I sighed.

"Seattle has been evacuated," Carrie said to the crowd.

"How do you know?" One man asked.

"It was on the news in Kamloops, this isn't a secret to the world anymore. It can't be contained," Celinde added.

"We need to go and save who we can, while we can," I ordered.

"ALL wolves will clear out of here, the women will stay," I glared at Graham.

"You want me to come and watch your back after you've just threatened to kill me?" he laughed.

"You came to me once seeking peace, you have a chance to redeem your wickedness. Work with me and we can find a middle ground between us," I pressed as eyes watched our exchange.

"Middle ground?" He queried; his eyes lit up.

"Yes," I nodded as I reached my hand to shake his.

"I'll watch your back, Dr. Collins, don't stab me in mine," he agreed and shook my hand.

The congregation became messy as everyone said their goodbyes and rummaged about food and supplies to bring with them.

V.J.Garland

CHAPTER NINE

CHRISTIAN

Jax had managed to broker peace with Graham's pack — for the meantime.

We traveled on foot and in our wolf forms down to Washington. The journey was rough. The snowstorm didn't cease for a single minute and that made hunting difficult, Tristan did his best and went after whatever he could with the help of Ezra and Austin.

It took us days to reach Washington and longer again once we had to travel as humans through the remaining populated areas, and everything was far denser due to the evacuations.

Jax tried to book us rooms in a town about an hour outside of Seattle to regroup and eat a decent meal.

"This hotel is full too," He cringed as he left the foyer.

"Let's try the campgrounds," I suggested.

We walked a while down the road till we found a busy camping ground, it was almost at capacity and full of families.

"They'll let us camp on the banks of the stream and had some sleeping bags for us," Austin cheered as he left the office with handfuls of sleeping bags hanging off his arms.

"Guess that's our five-star lodgings for the evening," I shrugged to the mass of men behind me.

There were close to forty of us in total, about ten women back at the Precinct. I knew they'd be okay under Carrie and Mindy's care.

The guy's setup up their sleeping bags all huddled together. This was far easier when we were out in the snowstorm away from people. We could sleep in our other forms, and we never felt the cold, but as humans, we felt everything with more severity. We looked like a bunch of hungover men still going through puberty.

It always amazed me that we had this excelled healing yet when it came to the barbed hair it would strip our skin right back for days, often leaving our faces raw and hideous.

A beard was the best way to hide it, but for those of us like myself who couldn't grow a full beard, it made it difficult. Ezra had it down to a fine art, his beard connected in all the right places even down past his neck. He embodied what it was to be a werewolf and carried himself so incredibly well.

Never tense, never presumptuous, but always alert and ready to act when called upon. He was eternally loyal.

"Why are you pining for me, Christian," Ezra laughed as he caught me in a glance.

"I'm just being an owl," I laughed.

"I see that...Your heads just rotating as you observe everyone without any thoughts," he laughed back.

"Where's Austin and Liam?" I asked.

"They went with Jax and Jake to get food," Ezra answered.

"Oh good! I'm famished," I grumbled.

"I'm so excited for a burger Mindy didn't make," he chuckled.

"That sounds too good to be true," I agreed.

"Hey!" Arthur growled.

"Just kidding, Art!" I slapped him on the back as he sat with us.

"Who am I kidding, I'd kill for a pizza that isn't from Costco or made by Mindy," he laughed.

"We are lucky to have her!!" Ezra added.

"We are, we'd be living on ramen noodles without the girls," I added.

"We'd have no chance at this partially normal life that's for sure," Graham sat beside Arthur and agreed.

"What's your story, Graham?" Ezra questioned.

"My story?" he asked.

"What's your beef with Jax?" I glowered.

"Maybe I'm just tired of struggling and living a week in one town and repeating that process till I have to jump states. Or I'm just jealous that he had it all figured out and created something positive," he sighed.

"Lycanthropy took everything from Jax, his girlfriend, his brother, his home, his career. Don't be so quick to judge, He struggles more than you know," I assured him.

"Kyle..." Tristan sighed as he sat down beside me.

"That was some sad shit," Jamal choked as he wrapped his sleeping bag around himself beside Ezra.

"It was awful," I sighed.

"Perhaps we've just misunderstood one another," Graham looked at me then at Ezra.

"Wish you'd have come to that epiphany before those girls hacked my arm off," Evan growled from behind.

"Stop complaining, you got it back," Graham laughed,

"It fucking hurt!" He scowled as he held his arm.

"I smell food—" I sniffed as I got up and followed my nose.

Jax and the others brought over four huge boxes full of burgers fries, pizza, drinks, and most importantly— beer!

"Tell me there's Guinness?" Ezra begged.

"Jake's box," Jax smiled.

"A real burger!" Tristan beamed with joy.

"PIZZA!" Arthur exasperated.

"Yeah, sorry. We cleaned them out of burgers," Liam apologized.

"No, I'm thrilled," Arthur took a whole pepperoni pizza, sat beside the bank, and devoured a full slice in two bites.

"How many burgers did you order?" asked Tristan.

"Well, I tried to order eighty, but they only had sixty so hence the pizzas," Jax replied.

"Hungry?" I laughed.

"It's been a tiring few days," he chuckled as he drank from a beer bottle.

"This could work out—with Graham," I nudged.

"It's not Graham I'm worried about, to be honest..." he sighed.

"Penny for your thoughts?" I asked.

"If every wolf can come back for a whole month every one hundred years, what does that mean for us? Even if we die, we'll never truly know peace..." he thought aloud.

"It means you get to find Joel and say goodbye and I get to tell Noah that Lupe is resting safely at the firehouse," I grasped his shoulder to reassure him.

"How do we find them?" I asked.

"You'll have to sniff them out," Graham came and stood with us.

"You've done this?" I asked.

"Evan isn't my only son," he explained.

"Evan's your son," Jax choked on his beer.

"He was only six when I turned, I waited till he and Tate were older and had lived a little before I came back for them. Tate didn't turn…" a tear built in his eye but quickly disappeared.

"Not everyone turns—" Jax sighed.

"I learned that the hard way," he shuffled his feet.

"I'm sorry, Graham," I held a beer out for him.

He took the beer and tipped it to the moon and took a hefty guzzle before letting out a loud burp.

"Who turned you?" I asked.

"Nobody. It was a sudden onset," he explained.

"Same as Noah—" Jax glared at me.

"Weird, that's only the second time I've heard of it," I said through a bite of my burger.

We all drank our beers and enjoyed our food and for the first time in a long time I felt at ease, there was no lingering tension and we all felt like one pack, there was no division lurking between the would-be leaders.

I missed Celinde, things between us weren't good, we knew there was no future for us yet there were others just starting out. Jax and Lucy were smitten, Tristan and Alexa were finally public and not hiding behind supposed hunting trips. Everyone was just walking their own paths now.

Seattle would be a huge hurdle; we were out to save anyone newly turned and destroy anyone non-compliant.

We scoffed our food and slept as well as we could on rocks and branches and as soon as camps stirred, we set off once again, it was only a few hours to Seattle if we traveled through the woods.

Jax suggested abandoning the cars we had stolen for the previous leg of the journey, there were families who needed them more and we handed over our keys to the campsite desk for those who needed them most.

The walk was long, long until we were safely out of human sight, then it was exciting and freeing, nothing stood in our way now, most of the state was evacuated and we bounded through trees and snowcapped mountains until we reached the outskirts of a city under attack.

Helicopters were open firing as beasts just like us fell from towering buildings and howls hurled through the air piercing our ears.

Jax ordered us back into our human forms and we marched up behind a convoy of army vehicles left abandoned.

"They still run," Tristan announced as he ran the ignition.

"Buckle up everyone," I nodded as the others filled the trucks.

"Windows down, we want wolves to smell our familiarity and we don't want humans firing at us," Jax ordered.

"Let's roll in, everyone be alert and ready for anything," I added.

We drove into Seattle over one of the only remaining bridges that was passable, some had been blocked with overturned cars, and others completely shattered and led to nothing but the water below.

The city became louder as we drove in, people taking cover behind buildings, some armed, some injured. There were bodies everywhere, hung from fire escapes, light posts, and electrical wires were strewn decoratively like Christmas ornaments. It was ugly and a cleanup that would take years if it were ever attempted at all.

"The activity seems to be moving on from here," Ezra commented as he stood through the bars and observed the movements around us.

"They moved south!" a woman yelled as she approached the convoy.

"How do you know?" I asked.

She didn't reply but she pointed to her ears and then looked up to an apartment with children waving out from the window.

"Get out of here and go north as soon as you can," I said as I handed her my backpack, it didn't have a lot, some old saltines, apples, and three slices of pizza that Arthur couldn't get through.

She bowed her head with thanks and quickly ran back to where her kids were.

"Jax…" I grabbed his shoulder as I pointed to a mob of men walking toward the convoy.

"Everyone out," Jax ordered.

We piled out as they approached. Some sniffed at us as they wandered by, mostly red-eyed, disruptive, and frenzied from overfeeding. Some scaled buildings with their claws as they searched for their next meal, and others smashed car windows just for the sake of it.

"Christian," Tristan whispered.

"I know…" I nodded as I kept my eyes on the apartment and the wolves getting closer to the woman and her two children.

"GO!" Jax ordered as Reggie raced Fred, Ezra, and Austin to the building. Another wolf had smashed a window and smelt the humans.

Ezra tore him out and threw him to the ground severing his spine as he fell onto a fire hydrant.

But others noticed and raced to his aid. Reggie met them halfway and threw off who he could, but others came from the roof.

Graham and Evan raced up, their ease into transformation brought the rest of us on the ground time to morph and fight back.

These wolves were far easier to put down than anyone could have anticipated, they were weaker, inexperienced, and high from the intense feeding.

Most scurried away like cockroaches the minute one of us approached them, others tried to show off their new fangs and dance around the idea of a fight, but once they realized we were organized they quickly backed down. We hoped that once this moon phase ended, they'd all revert or die off. Clarence seemed to be truthful when he said he didn't know the aftermath. One hundred years ago the werewolf population wasn't what it is now. Noah had mistakenly turned the wrong companion and his bloodlust had resulted in the mayhem we were facing off.

Chapter Ten

The Massacre of Seattle

(The day of the attack.)

It was a Friday afternoon and Elle visited her usual nail salon to get her nails done before meeting with friends for dinner. The owner had recently died and there was a strew of new employees while the owner's son Troy tried to manage the bookkeeping and keep the place running, he'd been active in the salon for years and was familiar with most of the regulars. He was young, in his mid-twenties, and diverting from college for yet another year.

Elle was the last in the shop, she had a newer employee working on her nails, a cringe-worthy set that left Elle feeling rather underwhelmed.

"Please go and pay," the lady smiled as she directed Elle to the counter once she had finished.

Elle assessed her hands, three nails were wonky, one finger had been skinned by the sanding tool, and another smudged.

"I'm not paying for this," Elle announced as she stormed down the stairs of the salon.

Her friend caught her in the street and headed to the restaurant they frequently visited every Friday night. Elle was visibly upset, and Grace addressed her mood.

"Are you okay?" Grace questioned.

"I just came off a week of nightshifts, I'm just feeling a little deflated, and then the new girl screwed up my nails," she said as she held out her hand.

"Woah! I hope you didn't pay for that," Grace expressed.

"I kind of stormed out, how will I ever go back after that," she sighed.

"Since when do you get fake nails?" Grace asked.

"I've got a vacation booked in Tulum for two weeks, I leave Sunday," she smiled as she glowed with the thought of it.

"Thanks for the invite!" Grace joked.

"Well, you could come. Nick was meant to come, but we broke up. If you can get the time off, I'd love the company. I can't imagine Tulum is much fun alone," she sighed.

"Aww Elle, let me see what I can do, I'd be happy to get out of dreary Seattle for a while!" she laughed.

They arrived at the restaurant where two other friends were already sitting waiting at their regular table, cocktails already in hand and garlic butter with fresh mini baguettes placed at each table setting.

"Finally!" Sam smiled as Grace and Elle took their seats and sipped their pre-ordered martinis.

"Sorry, disaster at the nail salon…" Elle sighed.

"My purple toner wasn't washing out," Grace grunted as she examined her long white hair.

"You still look beautiful, even if it's just for us," Sam clinked her glass to Grace's.

"Elle and Nick broke up—" Grace blurted.

Elle's hurt sank as she stuffed a buttered baguette in her mouth and lowered her eyes to play with her napkin.

"Sorry, it had to be said, we need to show you a good night!" Grace said as she hailed down a waiter and ordered a second round of drinks.

"I really just want a good dinner and a decent night of sleep, shift work is kicking my ass," she yawned.

Elle was a journalist at the Seattle Times and took the nightshift every second week or whenever nobody else wanted it. In truth it was a crappy shift, not much news that came through in the late evenings was good. Celebrity crisis stuff, cheating husbands, deaths, all the miserable things she hated gluing her name to publicly.
"What is all that noise?" Grace grumbled through a mouthful of fish.

"Must have been a car accident," Elle peaked through the windows on Pike Place.

"There's people running," Elle gasped as she turned back to the table and noticed an alarming number of phones ringing throughout the restaurant as panic and disorder took over.

"How many?" Grace questioned.

"Everyone…" Elle replied.

"We should go," Sam shouted as the restaurant began to empty.

"I'll go pay," One of the girls announced as she got up.

On the way to the counter, she was knocked down by the crowd and trampled beneath the feet of anxious patrons.

"Connie!" Sam yelled as she stood on a table looking for her.

People were now rushing in seeking shelter as others tried desperately to leave.

"What is going on, Elle?" Sam whimpered as they jumped to stand on the seating ledge.

"I'm not sure, Sammy, but we should get out of here. Where's Grace?" she asked.
"She went to help Connie," She look around the restaurant floor for them.

"DUCK!" Elle yelled as she grasped Connie and pulled her away from the window.

A motorcycle had driven through the window and taken out the driver and two other people.

"Call 911!" Sam screamed as she rushed to help the injured.

She threw herself back quickly in fear as she noticed something not right with the driver and tugged at Elle as she attempted first aid.

"Run!" Sam yelled at Elle.

Elle didn't question her, they beelined for the exit without a second thought and raced down the street seeking shelter.

Sam stopped two blocks down to take off her shoes.

"Come on, Sam. We need to get out of here," Elle urged.

"We need to ring Grace and Connie!" Sam stopped her. "Do you hear that?" Elle froze and looked around as silence ensued in the busy street of people as they also froze to listen.

Howling, louder, deeper snarls she'd never heard before. "What was wrong with that man back there, Sam?" Elle asked.

"His eyes— they weren't human…" she said.

"We need to move!" Elle gripped her wrist and dragged her down the road.

They ran another three blocks in bare feet and evening dresses. They reached the block where Elle had just had her nails done. It was quieter here; the panic hadn't stretched this far—yet.

"Up here," Elle whispered.

It was the stairway that led to the top floor of the building where she had just had her nails done.

Elle knocked gently. There was no answer, so she twisted the doorknob; it was unlocked.

"We shouldn't just go in there," Sam protested.

"We'll be safer up here than down there," she pointed down the stairway.

Sam sighed and agreed, they entered the salon. The lights were all switched off in the main areas and they proceeded to hide in the kitchen which doubled as a lunchroom.

"Who's there?" a man called. His footsteps got closer, and a light flickered on in the hallway.

"ELLE!" Troy yelled.
"Are you here to pay me the money you owe me?" he raged.

"You expect me to pay for this?" Elle walked closer to him and held her hands out.

"You should have told me! What are you doing here? I'm trying to sleep!" He growled and he let her hand loose.

"Sleep?" Sam laughed.

"Why is she laughing," he looked to Elle.

Elle shot her a glare as Sam began to perve on Troy's bare chest.

"Something is wrong out there…" Elle shivered at the thought.

"Like what?" Troy asked.

"It's chaos, people are going crazy, racing up and down streets, trampling one another and there's a sound. It's almost wolf-like," Sam explained.

Troy moved to a window at the side of the building and peered through the shutters.

Sounds of gunfire started and it was hard to tell what was happening anymore.

"We should barricade the doors," Troy said.

"Let's do that," Elle agreed as she raced around looking for heavy items.

Sam was covering windows upstairs while Elle and Troy went downstairs to block the doors.

"Why are you sleeping here?" Elle asked Troy.

He sighed as he took her in with his eyes and let out a deep breath.

"When mom died, she left me nothing except all her debt. I had to sell my house to cover it, the books said this business was thriving and the advice I got was to keep it going. It's not as easy as all that," he sighed.

"I shouldn't have stormed out without paying, I'll pay you back," Elle said sadly.

"No, she did a shit job, you don't have to," he shook his head as he chained the stairwell door closed.

"But I do need to fire her and find someone who didn't lie on their resume," He grumbled.

Elle smiled and nodded as she walked back up the stairs where Sam was on the phone to Grace.

"They're two blocks away, I'm going to bring them back here," Sam whispered as she climbed out to the fire escape stars.

"Sam! Be careful," Elle whispered out of the window.
"I will," she said.
"Elle," Troy called from the lunchroom where the TV was on.

Troy's phone buzzed with government warnings urging citizens to evacuate the city.

"What is going on?" Elle slumped into a chair.

Troy grabbed her by the hand and took her to the room he had been living in and threw sweatpants and a sweater at her.

"Put those on, you can't get around in that dress," he ordered.

But Elle was frozen and terrified of what she'd seen on the news. She'd seen reports coming out of Cannon Beach, Warrenton, and Astoria until they went silent, but the news called in something else, this was the first time they'd named it, werewolves — and they were rampant.

Troy tore at her dress and unzipped it from the back and slipped the sweater over her for cover.

"You need to do the pants!" He shook her.

"Werewolves?" she whispered.

The doors rattled and the chains thrashed against themselves, Elle sunk to the cover of the room and Troy drew a gun from his top drawer and listened for Sam below.

Elle pulled herself together at the thought of Sam and slipped the pants on as she raced after Troy.

Their eyes met and Troy motioned that he hadn't heard Sam, just passers-by or people being thrown into the building.

"She'd come up the fire escape," Elle whispered.

Troy nodded and agreed, and they moved back to the lunchroom where they had left the TV muted.

"Pack a bag," Troy passed her a backpack.

Elle began filling it with snacks, fruit, and anything in the fridge that could last a few days.

Troy had done the same and packed extra ammo for the gun along with some hunting tools.

"We'll give her an hour…" he looked to Elle whose face was washed white.

She took a seat at the table and watched as carnage enveloped Seattle and werewolves leaped from building to building and Helicopters filmed footage of the larger wolves hurling cars into the air trying to knock them out of trajectory.

"ELLE!" Sam's screams came from the side alley.

Her voice was panicked and fearful.

"Close the door!" Troy yelled as he watched over my head.
"I can't leave her there!" Elle rushed for the door, but Troy threw her back and pulled the blinds down.

But snarling and chomping filled their ears now, the sound of a werewolf devouring Sam from limb to limb and stripping her bones of everything, muscles, tendons, and flesh.

Elle wept into her hands and Troy pulled her to him as he tried to muffle her cries.

"Shhhhhh," he urged as he pulled her closer.

The sound of the wolf disappeared slowly, but they had traveled too far into the city to escape.

"We can't go on foot, we'll have to take the car," Troy said.

"What if the roads are blocked," Elle asked through her tears.

"We gave it our best shot," he said panicked.

"We need to go to ground zero, where the outbreak first happened," she suggested as she trotted down the stairs in shoes far too big for her.

Troy opened the garage to an old Toyota RAV4.

"You have an SUV?" Elle queried as she looked at Troy, he was no older than twenty-eight, over six foot tall, and build like a quarterback.

"It was moms like I said. I sold everything I had," he looked embarrassed as he opened the door for Elle.

"I wasn't mocking you; I was just a little surprised," she apologized.

Thuds were crashing into the garage door and the sounds of doors closing alerted the wolves lingering in the streets.

"Why ground zero?" Troy asked.

"Because none of them will be there now," She replied. It made sense, anything with that speed and hunger wasn't going to sit around and wait for food to come to *it.*

V.J.Garland

CHAPTER ELEVEN

CARRIE

I'd felt sick for days since the guys left, even before in Kamloops, something had been brewing in me, but I was too busy to address it. I wasn't sure if it was worry and fear or if I was actually unwell. It was constantly dark here at the Precinct. Unusual for this part of Canada. The only natural light came from the moon as it glowed red and beamed down to dance on the river that ran down the back of the cabins.

"Knock, knock!" Mindy banged against the cabin door where I had taken refuge.

"Come in," I said.

Mindy opened the door and Alexa bounded through with Lucy and Celinde.

"You don't look so good," Celinde grimaced.

"I feel like shit," I agreed.

Mindy was restocking the kitchen while Lucy bustled about tidying up my mess. Alexa was in the kitchen making tea.

"I really don't think I can socialize right now," I sighed as I lay back down in the bed.

"We aren't here for chit-chat, we just wanted to see that you are alright," Mindy objected.

"And keeping up your fluids, and taking something for the discomfort," Celinde handed me a large bottle of water and a box of painkillers.

"Thank you," I said with a forced smile.

"There must be something going around," Mindy shrugged.

"Oh?" I said aloud.

"Izzy's been feeling pretty under the weather and hasn't come out of her room in a few days. Said she's got something like a migraine, vomiting, and sensitivity to light. I just keep leaving food at her door," Mindy shrugged.

"Sounds a lot like what I have, maybe you guys should stay away from us encase it's contagious," I pressed trying to get them to leave.

"How can you be sensitive to light when there isn't any, that eclipse has been lurking for days…everything looks like blood," Celinde muttered as she ignored my plea and plopped herself beside me.

"Damn it! Lucy, must you run the dryer right now?" I growled.

"Sorry, maybe we should let her rest…" Lucy retreated to the front door.

I wanted to apologize, but something in me warned me not to extend the invitation for them to linger any longer. So, I sat silent while they each hurried about their task and quietly slipped out the front door of Ezra's cabin, but not before Celinde threw a blanket over me and coddled up on the sofa.

My body was weak, I could barely peel myself from the sofa. My skull felt like it was going to crack open, and my fingers were numb and paler than normal.

I knew what was happening the instant my jaw began to hurt. I was in transformation.

Ezra had explained it to me so many times and I'd overheard conversations between Christian, Jake, and Tristan describing how it felt — I wasn't ready.

All these years we thought we women got away with it, somehow being female made us immune, that only men were cursed and even then, *it* chose the men it inhibited. In theory, I should have changed years ago. I'd been scratched more times than I could count, and I had the scars to prove it. It became something of a kink between Ezra and me. The added element of danger kept our sex life alive, so alive that it's all we had in the end. We knew we had no lengthy future ahead, not together. We were living a whimsical life and I was just dangling in front of him keeping it interesting. That wasn't to say there was no love, no deeper emotions but I knew better than to let that lead my life.

Hours went by and my gums swelled, and as my gums swelled so did my face, my hair began to fall out and my skin cracked as it made room for things more insidious to evade it. My hands were frail, it hurt to clench them, it was arthritis-like but possibly worse. I hauled myself to the bed and used the emergency chains Ezra had kept to lock myself down. Only in time for my eyes to burn through my eyelids, all I could see was red and I felt the veins explode and take on a new form. I watched as my teeth were forced from my gums and landed on the floor only to be replaced by canines so sharp, they cut me as they forced their way out of a jaw still too small to house them.

A deep bellowing roar left me as the pain moved over my body, my skin tore as hard bristles ravaged my pale skin, my breasts flattened somewhat as muscles took over and bones moved and reanimated in ways I can't explain.

My hands were the worst of it, they'd hurt for hours before I was in full-fledged transformation. I heard every bone snap; I felt every bone grow unnaturally fast and watched as my skin struggled to keep up and contain my innards. Then hard calloused claws took over my poorly kept nails and poured blood from every finger and toe as I reveled in my new body.

The chains were tight — too tight.

I wracked them against the bed ignoring my better judgment, I wanted to be free, I wanted to feel the cold air on my back and bound through the field in seconds. I wanted to sink my teeth into a body that still beats and feel its attempt to fight me off.

There were low howls outside my cabin, soon accompanied by screams. I thrashed my chains harder, but they were bolted tight.

The door flung open and who I knew could only be Izzy tore the door handle off with her muzzle.

She paced hesitantly toward me; she was her own beast now too. Majestic and powerful. She tore at my chains until I was free and led me outside to the porch where we stood together as other wolves ran riot through Wolftown circling the well.

I could smell it from here, the poisonous aroma of liquid metal. Jax had filled the wells with the last of the colloidal silver. No wonder the guys always stayed far away from it. To us *humans*, it was a pool of urine-colored liquid. If a human bathed in it for too long, it would turn them permanently blue, however, it had incredible healing benefits. For the wolves, it would burn through us like a superacid. It was inevitably piranha solution for werewolves and just a droplet would burn for days.

Izzy licked her muzzle as she inhaled the scent of humans and looked around for the host of the tangible scent.

I looked down into the well, Alexa and Lucy were deep down in the colloidal holding on for their lives against the bricks.

Olivia could be heard in the woods behind the village, but not for long. Mindy got to her before she could pass the river.
"STOPPPP!" Alexa cried.

But there was no one to respond. Lucy was frozen in fear and Izzy teased as they began ripping bricks away slowly from the top of the well, taking her time to emit fear and torture.

Wolftown glowed red against the moon and the others unoccupied began to separate into the woods hunting for food. We'd starved ourselves for too long for this purpose — now we were the purpose.

CHAPTER TWELVE

AWAKENING

The ground rattled under the fire station setting off the alarms and waking the crew. The shaking continued and the sound of broken glass could be heard exploding as mugs, glasses and vases fell to the floor smashing them into fragments.

Lupe's urn teased the edge of a shelf through the shaking and burst into pieces mid-air without hitting the ground. Dave and the others raced in to find a sea of smashed glass and ceramic but no ashes. The ashes had floated past them, shaped as Lupina's face. The shaking continued and threw the men to the floor as a brisk breeze carried Lupe's ashes out of the station and into the nights air.

"You saw that?" Dave questioned himself and he leant back into Steve.

"I was afraid you didn't see it," he breathed a sigh of relief. "No time for that, there's going to be people who need help out there," the chief ordered.

"Earthquake?" Steve asked as he hauled himself up and into the truck.

"Something like that," the chief pursed his lips and secured his helmet onto his head.

Dave and the others were anxious and followed the glowing hue of dust that danced through the air, the dust that was once Lupina as it slowly grew as the moonlight gave her strength to rebirth.

The earth stood still, everything was underwhelmingly quiet as the trees settled, and the red hue darkened as life came back to her, still ghostly, transparent, and beautiful as ever. She cast a vague gaze at the truck as she stood in the road naked and bloody as her essence returned slowly.

"What in the fuckery is happening?" The chief gasped.

"I have no idea…" Dave whispered; he couldn't tear his eyes away.

Lupe's eyes darkened as her rebirth came full circle, rain began to beat down heavily, and Dave raced outside and threw his jacket around her.

"Lupe? I thought you were dead?" he questioned as he carried her into the truck and sat her beside Steve who now looked sickly.

But she didn't respond. Her body was icy to the touch and lacked any responsiveness.

"I'll drive, you check her out," the chief ordered. He turned the truck around and headed towards a hospital.

"NO!" Lupe screamed with a screeching pitch.

"Calm down, Lupe. You're safe, we won't let anyone hurt you," Dave tried to calm her.

"Take me back, take me to Cannon Beach!" She ordered.

"Lupe, that's nine hours away!" the chief argued.

She whipped the door open and leapt from the cab racing off into the darkness.

"We can't just let her run off—naked!" Dave croaked at the chief.

"She's been traumatized by something," Steve added as he rubbed his stomach in discomfort.

"I'm going after her, she won't get far on foot," Dave announced as the truck pulled back into the fire station.

"What about the earthquake?" Steve asked.

"Did you see anything out there that indicated we had just been hit by a serious earthquake?" Dave questioned.

"There's nothing coming in on the radio, the TV isn't reporting anything either," he stood and pointed the news reporting on baseball through the window.

"Go and get her, bring her back her!" The chief ordered.

Dave, Steve, and Trent piled into Steve's RAM and sped off into the night down the same road Lupe had ran towards.

"That was some hocus pocus shit, right?" Trent asked with a nervous tone.

"I don't know what that was, but I do know that's our buddies supposedly dead wife racing off naked between the two states with the second highest bear counts behind Alaska," Dave grumbled.

"Well, you better speed then!" Trent smiled and nudged Steve.

"There's no way she got this far already; we were only minutes behind her," Dave pondered.

"I don't see anything," Trent sighed as he peered through the windows.

They drove a few more miles and stopped to climb up onto the car and shine the spotlights through the woods.

"She's got to be out here somewhere..." Dave growled.

"Or she's somethings dinner.," Trent joked.

Steve darted him a less-than-impressed glare.

"Oh, come on! Have a laugh," Trent chuckled.

"Bloody Rookie! You didn't know Lupe like we did, you didn't know Noah. This isn't like her," Dave groaned.

"Didn't know her? She's sat on that shelf the last three months I've been in this godforsaken town watching me eat breakfast and scratch my balls... we're well acquainted," Trent cackled.

A loud thud slammed against the truck and Trent was ripped down from the tray and slammed into the ground, blood billowing from his mouth as he coughed through the immediate drowning. Dave and Steve looked around and Lupe was removing his clothes and pulling them over herself.

"Miss me?" She smiled, she had more color to her now, a chin covered in blood and eyes dark as ever.

"Did you do that?" Steve protested.

"No! It was that bear…" She lied as she pointed to a bear she had been snacking on and dragged into the road, it was still conscious, but fearful of Lupe.

"She's half his size, Steve! How could she?" Dave was on her side.

"Call in the medic to grab this guy," Steve ordered Dave.

They waited around for a few minutes while the medics beamed their way with lights flashing, they collected Trent's body and tended to him as best they could, but it was too late.

Lupe climbed into the truck and sat quietly in one corner as she collected herself. She was confused and thrown years ahead of her death.

"Why Cannon Beach?" Dave asked as he climbed into the truck.

"That's where they'll be…" she sighed.

"Who?" Dave asked.

"Everyone," she answered.

"Lupe, it's a whole day's drive, are you sure?" Steve asked.

"It's all I'm sure of…" she sunk her head into the seatbelt and closed her eyes as she bathed in the warmth from the vent blowing out hot air.

Dave and Steve took turns driving so they got there in good time. The town was empty, still abandoned and shut off from the world, but not free of its monsters.

"Let me out here, you should go home," Lupe pressed.

"Where will you go?" Dave asked.

"Trust me, I'm going to be fine. I'll find a way to send word to you," she smiled.

"I wish I could explain," she added as she held Dave's hand.

"Take care, Lupina," Steve said with a salute as he drove off down the highway.

Lupe walked down towards the beach and sat in the sand beneath the moonlight and listened as other wolves howled from the coastline as they all drank in the eclipse's magic.

Hours passed by and Lupe dove into the sea to wash her body free from the blood of the bear and Trent. She emerged from the waves with a large halibut in her clutches, claws ripping through it, and red hungry eyes that glowed.

"Caught your second Halibut?" a deep and familiar voice whispered through a smile.

Lupe looked around, but there wasn't anyone on the beach, werewolf, or human.

"Come out!" She growled as she let the halibut fall to one side of her.

"Look up," The voice commanded.

Noah was perched upon the larger of the rocks gazing down at Lupe.

"I knew I'd find you here," she smiled as she climbed up the rocks.

"Clothes?" He questioned.

"Ughh, I'm meant to be dead. Fuck the clothes," She laughed as she scaled the rocks with ease and launched herself at him.

Noah held her tightly and brushed the wet hair from her face and cold fish scales from her chin.

"How are we here? how did I know to find you here?" She asked.

"I don't know, maybe it's a dream," he smiled.

"I'm like you now? How?" She questioned as she held out her swollen red hands.

"That's what we need to find out, I have a feeling this is all connected," Noah sighed as she took her hands in his and held them.

"What is?" Lupe asked.

"All of this," Noah looked up to the eclipse.

"HEYYYYY!! LUPE," Joel called from the beach.

"It's Joel!!!" Lupe leaped down in a single leap into the water and landed with perfect ease and raced towards Joel, tackling him in a hug.

"Okay, seriously! CLOTHES!" Noah snarled as he followed her.

Noah removed his shirt and threw it over Lupe exposing his bare chest and Joel couldn't tear his eyes away.

"That's your husband…" Joel whispered to Lupe.

Lupe smiled and nodded as the three of them walked towards the path that led to the street.

"He's ruggedly handsome," Joel laughed.

"I know," Lupe laughed back as she felt comfortable with her old friend.

"I can hear you…" Noah grunted.

Noah walked past empty homes and peered through broken windows.

"Here, this house looks mostly untouched," he said as he directed Lupe to an open window.

"I'm not going in there…" she hissed.

"I'll go," Joel winked jokingly.

"There're other wolves around, and they aren't all nice. My guess is if we can all come back, there's going to be more of us. You need clothes," he pressed as he cornered her into a wall.

The sexual tension between them was ripe and Joel was fanning himself dramatically with his hands as he watched on before Noah darted him a glare that made him retreat to a bedroom within the small home.

"Be nice, he likes to joke!" Lupe pushed Noah back.

Lupe brushed passed Noah and met Joel in the hall as he handed her a pair of cargo pants, sneakers, and a long sleeve thermal top. She went into the room to dress while Noah stood over Joel intimidating him with his immense stature.

Joel held out his hand to shake Noah's. Noah barred his teeth and let Joel shake his hand.

"I'll try to behave," Joel nodded.

"That would be appreciated," Noah relaxed and unclenched his body.

"Now what?" Lupe growled as she stormed out of the room fully dressed.

Tires could be heard screeching down the street, far closer than where Dave and Steve had dropped her off. Wolves began to howl, and car sirens went off as concrete cracked from the shaking.

"What is that?" Joel whispered.

"Hopefully, not Jerry," Noah sighed.

Three army vehicles began to roll through followed by three more civilian trucks and men began to roll out with hoses ready to plug them into a fire truck abandoned on the side of the road.

"Stay here..." Noah held Lupe's face and kissed her gently.

"Noah, you don't know who they are!" Lupe objected.

"They aren't human, look at their eyes...lots of yellow and white. We're in good company," he released her and bounded for the door before she could speak. Joel held her back and they watched on from the window.

Noah approached the fire truck and seemingly recognized it as he went to check the number plates.

"No way!" he muttered.

"CHRISTIAN!" Noah shouted as Christian appeared from around a corner.

"NOAH!" Christian raced for Noah and caught him in a hug as the others emerged from behind more vehicles.

"How?" Christian asked.

"I don't know, but it can't be good. Lupe's here too," He added.

"Lupe?" Jax stepped forward and asked.

"You're the boyfriend?" Noah puffed his chest as he asked.

"You're the husband?" Jax smiled.

Noah nodded as he looked over to the cottage-styled home where Lupe was tumbling out of a window.

"Jax?" She called from the street as she began to run.

She leaped into him and hugged him tightly. Joel was steps behind her, and he added himself to the pile and wrapped his arms around them both.

"You guys are alive!" Jax wept.

"No, they aren't alive, they are caught in the moon cycle," Ezra began to explain as he stood tall beside Noah.

"Who's this guy?" Noah asked.

"He's old," Jax answered.

"Not as old as me," Graham chimed in as he looked Lupina up and down. Clarence scoffed to challenge them both with his extraordinary age.

Graham grabbed Lupina by the shoulders and looked her over, his expression confused.

"Well, that's not good," he sighed.

"What?" Lupe asked as she brushed him off her and stood between Noah and Christian.

Graham's expression was puzzled as he thought long and hard as he unloaded thoughts at Clarence with his eyes.

"Were you scratched? Bitten? Did you survive an attack?" Graham pressed.

Lupe lifted her leg and exposed a large scar. Noah sighed as he wrapped his arms around her chest and held her close to him and she held onto his forearms.

"That's bad," Christian gasped.

"Why?" Joel grumbled.

"Lucy," Jax shrieked.

"Oh shit!" Ezra piled into a car and hollered for everyone to load up.

"Guess we're taking the fire truck," Noah sighed.

"I'll go with them and explain," Jax yelled back. Christian followed him and they all loaded up into the truck.

Christian took the driver's seat while Ezra clung onto the back with Jake and Tristan pulling up the hoses.

"Long story short, all this werewolf stuff got crazy. We created a home in the middle of nowhere with all of our human wives and girlfriends and some of them got hurt over the years—accidentally. Some did not," Jax explained.

"And you're worried they came back like me?" Lupe questioned.

"Well, you were dead. Maybe it's different, but we need to be sure," Christian replied.

Ezra pounded on the roof as the other cars began to slow down.

"What's going on?" Joel asked.

Noah leaped from the truck and walked to the edge of the light beams, he was met with eyes, red eyes and bulking bodies, snarls crisp and snapping at him as he let his body release its power, he was equally as big as Jax in his beast form, he towered over eight feet tall and wore scars that aged him. Christian and Jax were close behind him and the other wolves began gnashing and scrapping at the ground, eager to pounce.

"Get up here both of you and grab a hose. Don't get this on yourselves..." Tristan ordered.

"What is it?" Joel asked.

"Colloidal silver," Jake answered.

Joel and Lupe looked at one another and shrugged their shoulders as they held the hoses tightly.

"Go easy, there's only a third of a tank," Ezra whispered.

"Who is that?" Tristan asked Joel as Noah stood over a balding werewolf.

"That's Noah's nemesis," Joel answered.

"Didn't he kill you?" Lupe said as she looked at Joel.

"Yep," Joel snarled as he barred his teeth for the first time.

"Jake…" Tristan grasped his wristed and Tristan watched another group of wolves closing around them.

"Austin!" Jake yelled.

Austin and Liam stopped at the back of the truck with Arthur and Henry as Tristan's two brothers and Wesley's wolves approached the convoy.

"If you have a plan, Jax. Do it now!" Ezra yelled.

Jax and Noah locked eyes, and tore through Jerry and Maverick, dust and blood flew in every direction as the other group advanced on the others.

"Here we go again," Tristan sighed as he prepped his hose.

Lupe and Joel copied and found targets to aim at.

"FIRE!" Ezra ordered as he released the valve.

Werewolves flew in every direction as the force of the colloidal split one wolf down the middle, his body fizzled as his advanced healing dared to fight the liquid with no hope.

"Good shot!" Lupe high-fived Joel.

"We aren't done yet," Jake barked as Ezra and Tristan morphed slowly and jumped down with ease onto the ground and they plowed through old enemies.

"Noah and Jax need help," Lupe grasped Joel.

"I don't know how to do that…" Joel whispered.

"Neither, just feel it, like a poop?" she glanced with playful eyes and squeezed Joel's hand until her claws were out and penetrating his hand. His eyes lit up at her humor and he concentrated hard on his transformation.

Lupe's fangs were long and sharp, eyes yellow, muddled with orange, and slightly bloody, Joel's eyes were white and fearful as he bounded down from the truck and raced towards Jerry landing a hard blow to his muzzle and Jax held him down to let Joel continue.

Lupe raced after Lucas between the dark tree lines, he teased her with his experience and tested her skills as he shook and flung every tree, she rested in. She fell to the ground and rose from the mud to uproot a tree. She snapped it in half and launched it at Lucas with all her might like a javelin. It pierced him directly through the neck, the trunk of the tree so thick the body decapitated itself with the weight of Lucas's body dropping to the forest floor.

She approached the body; the hunger had found her, and the scent of blood became provocative to her.

Jax raced for her and held her back away from the body and pushed her away. He morphed back quicker than he ever had before and stood in her way as she towered over him.

"Don't go there Lupe, that's too dark, even after what you've lived through," he said calmingly.

"They need us!" He tried desperately to redirect her hunger and she snapped her muzzle at his face.

She pulled back as she saw Noah struggling against two other wolves and raced to his aid.

Tristan was at odds between Mike and Seb, Arthur and Henry held them back as Otis and Jamal covered fishing knives in the remaining colloidal and handed one to Tristan. Otis tore the blade down the back of Seb, embedding the colloidal so deep he'd never revive.

Mike let out a howl and morphed back into his young human self, curling into a ball of despair and Tristan took mercy on his little brother.

"Mikey?" Tristan met his level and tried to console him.

"HUMANS!" Jax yelled as headlights poured into the street and the wolves dispersed. All but Jax, Mike, and Tristan.

Troy hopped out of the SUV and approached Mike.

"Hey, do you guys need some help? It's not safe out here..." he shivered and rubbed his arms.

"Get out of here dude," Jax approached and tried to shew him away.

"Yeah, fuck off!" Mike replied as his gaze became twisted.

"Sorry, you just looked like you might need some help," Troy shook his head and began to walk back to Elle waiting patiently in the car.

"You need help, weak human!" Mike launched for Troy and buried his fangs deep into his back. His bones could be heard shattering.

Elle's screams echoed so sharply you'd have heard it back in Warrenton. Jax raced to help Troy.

Tristan took the blade and tore it across Mike's throat several times severing his head from his body before jumping onto the triple and dropping the head into the tank. He took a deep breath and panted heavily. Arthur jumped up with him and held him tightly as tears poured from his eyes and his heart visibly broke all over again.

"Oh, shit…" Noah sighed as he approached with a blood-covered Lupina.

Jax was trying to stop Troy's bleeding as Elle thrashed around in the car hysterically.

"I can't do this," Tristan cried.

"Trist, they were already dead. You had to protect yourself," Ezra tried to console him.

"I love Alexa… she's been the only good thing in my life, please tell her Arthur," Tristan stood up on the truck and held the blade while he thought for a short moment.

Arthur grabbed his ankle as tears built in his eyes.

"You can tell her yourself," Arthur smiled up at Tristan.

"I'm not coming home…" he bent down and held Arthur's hand.

"You've been the father I should have had," Tristan released his hand and exchanged a gaze with all his friends as they emerged from the woods, Jake rushed to the truck desperately, but he was too slow. Tristan threw himself into the tank and sizzling and screams pierced the air.

"NOOOO!" Jake clawed at the side of the tank and tore it open.

"Jake!" Jamal ripped him away from the colloidal as fast as he could, but his hands were already burning.

Jax rushed over with a bottle of water and tried to rinse the colloidal off, but it was sticking and eating away at Jake's flesh.

"Oh fuck," Joel sobbed as he pulled his eyes away and dropped to the ground in fear.

Elle's screaming knew no bounds as she wailed in the car completely wracked with fear, Troy lay across the bonnet as his body began to reanimate and spring back to life.

"WHAT THE FUCK ARE YOU?" Elle screamed.

"Shut her up…" Jake snarled.

Lupe walked to the car and grabbed Troy from the bonnet and lay him on the side of the road. Liam and Austin were mostly clean and humanlike, they climbed into the car with her trying to calm her before Jake made a meal out of her.

"We should go…" Jax urged.

"Where? Lupe asked.

"Home," he replied.

"Home?" She growled.

"We have a safe place to go, away from cities," he explained.

"It sounds like all you did was recreate what Noah and I had but it's a hundred times bigger…" she scowled.

"It almost is, it's not a perfect system, obviously neither was yours," Jax snapped.

Lupina backed off and retreated to Noah while Joel consoled Jax. He was close to Tristan and helped him better himself in a time when he was out of control.

CHAPTER THIRTEEN

NOAH

We ditched the triple, at least I got one last ride. Christian was quiet for most of the ride, the entire state of Washington had been declared a dead zone, which was an absolute lie on the government's behalf. But it was in fact deadly to be in, there were werewolves everywhere, most past the point of no return. Lupe was visibly afraid for Elle. Her caring nature sparked through, and she took it upon herself to sit with Elle in the SUV with Liam and Austin while Troy rode with us while he healed, and we could explain what was happening once his mind was clear.

Driving along we stumbled upon Cory, he was confused and slightly unaware of where he was.

"Cory," I said as I slowed beside him.
"Shit, Noah?" He beamed.

"Get in…" I brought the car to a stop while he piled into the front passenger seat.

"What the hell is going on?" Cory asked.

"Wish I knew buddy, you just missed all the action," I nudged him.

"Aren't we dead? I remember dying?" he questioned. "There's some sort of time loop, moon phase. We're back but not forever," I sighed.

"You'd want to be back forever?" He questioned.

"Lupe found me, she's alive and a werewolf, and I..." I couldn't finish my sentence.

"I understand brother, you want to make amends, you want your wife back," he smiled.

"Wasn't Lupe with Jax?" Liam interrupted.

"Not after she died, he's with Lucy now," Austin interjected.

"Are they a thing?" Liam asked.

"Yeah, apparently he was hiding her in his cabin, and it was a whole thing, that's why Graham went mental," Austin explained.

"Gossipy women back there," I laughed as Cory chuckled at their exchange.

"Sorry, it's been a busy week. Nobody knows what's going on in everyone's lives anymore," Austin laughed.

"How is Lupe?" Cory asked.

"Honestly, such a badass, but I know she'll be struggling, she almost fed tonight…" I sighed.

Troy began to shift in his seat, he snapped upright still dazed and confused.
"And now we're bringing new puppies along for the ride?" Cory snickered as he grimaced at Troy flinching in the backseat.

"He hasn't fed, we can't just leave him out there with no chance at a normal life," Liam argued.

"Normal life…" Cory scoffed.

"There's no such thing," I murmured.

Liam and Austin sat in silence and stared at me darkly in the rear-view mirror with no exchange of words, their arms held Troy down for the longest leg of the journey to the Precinct.

"Hey, I think we're stopping," Liam blinked tiredly after falling asleep on Troy.

"There's a Walmart," I said.

"Where are we?" Troy asked.

"Canada," Cory answered.

"How long were we asleep," Austin rubbed his red sore eyes.

"Five hours, give or take," I replied.

We all stepped out of the car and walked to the doors of the store to meet the others.

"Why are we here?" I asked Lupe.
"We all need to eat," she nodded as her stomach growled.

"The store looks empty," Jax said as he peered around inside.

"Free for all!" Joel clapped.

"Let's go," Lupe snatched his arm and beelined for the shopping carts.

"One each," Joel winked as Lupe laughed.

She was colder than normal towards me; I couldn't figure it out. We had this time together to fix what was broken and she wasn't warm at all, she was detached.

"Everyone should buddy up," Jax ordered.

"Partner?" Jax smiled at me.

"Cause that's not weird at all," I laughed as I pushed a cart along beside him.

"Relax, I'm not after your wife, I promise. I'm invested elsewhere," Jax smiled.

"Comforting," I smiled back.

"She's been off," I whispered.

"Give her time, she's never been a werewolf before. This is new for her," Jax suggested.

"Time is something I don't have a lot of," I sighed.

Jax pressed three large packets of bacon at me, and I tried to keep up as he kept passing me new items.
Eggs, pancake batter, butter, milk, and fruit.
Ezra and Christian were loading trolleys full of meat, more eggs, and bread.

"What the hell," I chuffed.

"The Precinct is running low on supplies," Jax sighed.

"So, your perfectly oiled machine isn't running so well," I asked.

"It never runs smoothly, we always ran out of food," he admitted.

"The answer to that problem...Frozen lasagna," Lupe snickered as she and Joel rolled past with a cart full of clothes.

"Well for a matter of fact..." Christian hollered.

"SHUT UP CHRISTIAN!" Jax growled playfully.
"Oh... you didn't!" Lupe laughed.

"You used to tease the shit out of me for eating frozen meals, how does it feel to fall from grace?" She cackled.
I backed away as they all poked fun at one another, and I went to collect shelf-stable items with the other empty cart.

"Don't tell me you're jealous of Jax," Graham crept up behind me.

"Not at all," I replied.

"You could take him, I saw you. You're just a big...bigger!" He tried to plant a seed of doubt, but I wasn't budging.

"They're friends, Graham. He took care of her when I couldn't, what do you want from me?" I asked.

"I just like making new friends! It makes sense for us to be friends, this life chose us... the rest of them are a product of our suffering, they're cheap copies," he smiled.

"Well, we're all in this together now," I nodded down at him.

He glared at me as I moved on to continue filling my cart and Lupe raced after me and clutched my arm.
I looked into her eyes and she blinked tightly for moments a little too long and held my arm closer.

"Sorry Noah," She sighed.

"Don't worry about it," I kissed her forehead.

"No, I mean it. Jax told me and you're right. This has been weird; I don't feel like myself at all. I don't like this version of me," she sighed.

"You haven't exactly had it easy Lupe, that's been my fault," I sighed.

"To be fair, you did try and make me leave you," she smiled and wrapped her arms around my ribs.

"Thank you for not leaving me, this is a lonely life at times," I squeezed her into me.

"Well, we've got something like three weeks to make up for lost time," she sighed.

I laughed as I kissed her and everyone around us clapped and cheered. But it wasn't the same, I felt resistance in her affections.

"Alright, back to your shoplifting," I laughed.

Christian and Jax lingered a little longer and nudged each other playfully.

"They seem quite close," Lupe observed.

"Besties!" Ezra said over the freezers.

"That is when Jax isn't locking himself away from everyone for weeks, sometimes months," he sighed.

"Why?" Lupe asked.

"I wasn't there when it happened, but he overstepped once, went full cannibal werewolf, and shredded a pack to their bones, I met him after that. He was okay but the PTSD still haunts him, then his human best friend went mental, he put him down too and that's the short version of why nobody messes with him," he peered over racks of clothes as he finished his whispers.

"Jax? We're talking about the same guy, right?" Lupe questioned.
"It took your husband, didn't it?" Ezra asked and pointed to me.

She sighed as she looked me up and down and stroked my forearm.

"Come on, let's get this done and get out of here," I urged.

Lupe followed behind me slowly. Ezra was explaining every detail about the Precinct, its inner workings, and how they had tried to maintain a balanced life out there. How their relationships were challenged, and they had recently tried to cut their human partners out and force them back into the real world.

Ezra was chirpy, fun, huge, and had this incredible warmth to his personality, he looked intimidating, his beard was ragged and scruffy, his hair was long with the odd natural dreadlock, and he had scars and random tattoos all over him.

Joel sped over with a cart full of plush towels and toiletries and purposely smashed into my cart.

"Shower anybody?" he winked.

"This guy is a werewolf?" I chuckled as I pressed my brows together with doubt.

"Sorry I don't fit the typical masculine werewolf stereotype, Noah!" he flipped me off as he pulled his cart back.

"Let's go find a shower," Lupe agreed as she began to scratch at her poorly healed skin.

"She needs to avoid turning...she'll start looking like us if she doesn't," Ezra held up his arms and looked at mine.

They were littered with keloid scars and blisters from ingrown bristles.

"Ah yes, lycanthropy is far from glamorous," Graham agreed, and he pulled his shirt open.

His scars had scars, and not just from his traumatic transformations, he had claw marks of various sizes strewn across his back and chest in thick shiny markings, proof of a life of fighting.

"What's that?" Jax asked as he curiously looked over Graham's chest and back.

"Which one…" Graham asked.

"That black brand," Jax replied.

"Mark of an original werewolf, one born, not bitten," he replied.

"I don't have that?" I mused.

"And you won't unless you are marked by a witch," he answered.

"Brands don't stick, human injuries don't mark, only what we do to one another, it's a reminder that we are chaos…the physicality of mayhem and uproar," Clarence added as he exposed his brand.
"Why?" I asked as I pondered the reality of witchcraft.
"Because those bitches have nothing better to do than cook up mischief!" Clarence chuckled.

"Witches?" Jax laughed.

"A real witch will strike you down and rip your wolf from your body, but you'll never find one. They are meant to keep the balance, that's how we've gone undetected for so long." Clarence explained as he sunk into a camping chair.

"Then why wasn't I marked?" I asked.

"You lived in confinement, you weren't overexposing yourself," Graham nodded.

"But why originals, why not everyone else?" I asked.

"...supernatural police if you will, they'll never kill off a natural-born werewolf, they can't do that. Only what comes from us," Graham answered.

"Dare I ask what else exists out there..." Ezra asked curiously.

"Too much, if you live long enough, and you'll find out for yourself," Clarence sighed.

"Vampires?" Ezra asked.

"Like you wouldn't even believe..." Graham answered.

"Tell me more!" Ezra's eyes popped from his skull eager for more.

"There's not a lot to tell, only two true vampires are remaining in the world, and they don't appear as you'd expect, they can be giant winged batlike creatures at times, others they are almost petrified mummies, and the bat form is unlike anything you'll ever lay your eyes on, huge winged ugly creatures," Clarence explained.

"So not our enemies? Damn!" Ezra joked.

"I'd love to see you up against a bat," I laughed.

"I can take a bat," Ezra pumped me playfully in the arm with his fist.

"Is there any food," Elle asked as she crept up wrapping a blanket around herself.

Jake tossed her a premade sandwich and some Jell-O. "Thanks," she sunk to the ground and began eating.

"Lupe's gone to find some showers if you wanted one," Jax urged.

"Once I'm done..." she waved her remaining half sandwich in the air.

"So, population-wise... who is in the lead?" Ezra asked.

"Sirens, maybe werewolves now... we used to be a quiet race, only taking what we needed when we needed," he rolled his eyes at me.

"Woah, you mean like mermaids?" Elle questioned.

"It's best not to talk about these things too much, speaking about them only breathes more life into such things," Clarence pressed.

"But they're already real!" Elle argued.

"And you are still a human, ready for snacking on. I'd be careful what you go hunting for in the night if I were you," Clarence sighed.

Elle chewed her last mouthful of sandwich with attitude and glared towards Clarence and then she hopped up and went looking for the bathroom.

"Why even tell her if you don't want her to ask, of course, she's going to ask," Ezra questioned.

"Because if she is busy thinking about that, it's less time for her to be afraid of us. She needs a distraction to busy her mind" Clarence sighed.

"Are they real though?" Ezra whispered.

"Never seen one in my life," Clarence laughed.

Ezra gently punched him in the shoulder and gaffed at how gullible he had been.

"Witches though?" I asked.

"Not pretty ones, and not ones who fly on broomsticks either. But they do exist," he nodded.

"When can we get out of here?" Jax asked.

"Not into superstition?" I asked.

"I'm still trying to swallow the werewolf stuff, I'll take it as I see it," he said.

He wasn't wrong, the werewolf stuff was heavy. If you were turned long enough you might be lucky to get away with memory loss, and splotchy darkness in places where you knew damn well there was blood and disorder, but thanks to the splotches you didn't have to relive the whole thing, you could get away with brushing it off and if there were no survivors you were extra lucky and in a sense that one turn didn't feel so bad even if it lasted for days.

The girls came out of the bathroom clean and fresh, they almost seemed friendly toward one another— almost.

I could see Lupe biting her lip as she tried so hard not to make a meal out of Elle but also doing her best to be cool and calm.

"Time to head out folks," Jax announced.

He was the embodiment of leadership, the others seemed to respect him. I felt a sense of relief as I thought back to my time in a pack of half-wits and Jerry at the helm doing all he could to undermine my authority. Graham and Clarence were sketchy characters, I didn't trust a word they said and tried my best to keep my distance between us, but they were always watching me.

Lupe jumped in the same car as me and we kept on the path to the Precinct.

"How far?" Lupe asked.

"I'm not sure, Jax said it was past Kamloops," I replied.

"Ughh, I hate long drives," she muttered.

"I know," I laughed as I reached my hand out to hold hers.

But she left me hanging as she tried to hold my gaze from the road.

"What?" I asked.

"I know what you're trying to do, Noah. Trying to fix us with however many days we may have left here, but it's not going to happen," she grumbled.

"Why?" I sighed.

"Well, which part do you want first?" she asked.

I knew I was in for an earful, she had years of pent-up anger and trauma and I deserved every part of it.

"Dish me up…" I sighed.

"The part where you tried to kill me, not once but a few thousand times," she growled.

"Thousands? I think you're exaggerating a little bit…" I said.

"NO, I AM NOT!" she yelled.
"How many days are in a year Noah? 365! Now times that by five and add some change…" she groaned.

"Okay…" I swallowed hard.

"And let's forget all the minor details and throw in the part where YOU left ME! You went on your merry way and thought I could just pick up where I left off! You sick son of a bitch!" She screamed.

"You were better off without me!" I argued.

"I was empty and alone without you Noah… I would have lived a hundred more years in fear of you than without you," she cried.

"I thought I was helping you…" I apologized.

"Helping me would have been killing me… what you did was worse," she wiped her eyes.

"You couldn't have helped me, Lupe," I gushed.

"I was willing to try," she locked my eyes.

"I'm sorry, I really am," I shed a tear.

'I can't even accept that, that would be making you apologize for who you are, this is what you were born to be…I love you, but I don't love this part of you," Lupe slumped back into her chair.

"What about you?" I asked.

"What about me?" she hissed.
"Do you hate what you are now?" I asked with caution.

"I wish I had stayed dead," She cried.

I couldn't respond to that; I was glad I was back. I hadn't missed any part of this life except her. There was nothing good *to* miss— just Lupe. And she hated me…
We sat for hours in the car silent, I watched between her and the road as she picked at her nailbeds until they were bloodied but I dare not say a word.

The roads were getting rougher and the air cooler as we rode up through mountainous dirt roads.

Jax slowed to a stop and climbed out of the vehicle.

"We need to move these trees off the road," he motioned for help.

"Off you go big guy," Lupe slapped me in the arm sarcastically.

There were countless trees littered over the roads, what looked like debris from a storm.

"Faster if we...y'know?" Arthur wiggly his hand to suggest we change our forms.

"Point taken," Jax nodded.

Most helped unless they were driving the cars behind us as we swept the road clear. It took under an hour, and we finally had a clear path to the Precinct. It was an eerily unusual place. We reached the opposite side from the bunker that looked down into the valley where a village of small homes was tightly connected.
"Wolftown!" Arthur smiled as he hurried down.

"Wait..." Jax stopped him. His eyes were suddenly yellow, a sign of his good intent and sense of humanity.

"Something isn't right here," Jake agreed.

Bats circled over the village and the red from the moon made all sources of water look like blood. Screams and erratic breathing were coming from a well or tunnel and Jax took to his beast form and bounded toward the sounds.

Graham snickered at me and launched down the hill next.

"What's going on?" Lupe asked.

"Nothing good," I held her gaze.

She ran down the hill with Elle and I carried Troy on my back.

When we made it to Wolftown Jax was standing off between others, all female, and trying to calm them down. He had hurled Elle into the well with Alexa and Kitty.

"Carrie, this isn't you. You need to calm down," Jax's pleas went unnoticed, and she licked her lips and drooled wildly into the well.

"If you go down there, you're dead," Jax growled.
"One more best friend you won't have to worry about..."
She scowled, her hands were bloodied from clawing at the well.

"That's not fair!" Ezra growled in Jax's defense.

"JAX! GET ME OUT OF HERE!" Lucy screamed.

"I'm trying," He looked down the well.

"What the fuck have you done here!" Lupe growled as she tore at the bricks on the well.

"NO LUPE!" Jax growled as he lunged for her and knocked her aside.

"Don't ever do that again," I growled at Jax as I pulled Lupe up from the mud.

"If that liquid touches her, it'll burn her, enough will kill her. Do you remember what happened to that boy back at Cannon, that's the same stuff!" He yelled as he walked away from us.

"What boy?" a crackly voice yelled from the bottom of the well.

"Alexa, we need to talk," Arthur began...

"WHERE IS TRISTAN?" Alexa yelled as the liquid around her thrashed.

She could be heard climbing the bricks, I could smell the blood from her grazes, the sound of her teeth chattering as they fought the cold.
Most of the men were holding the women back while she emerged onto the edge of the well.

Lupe's nose stifled in confusion as the hunger mixed with fear of the substance coating her body. She was blue and I wasn't sure if it were from the colloidal or the cold.

"Mom!" She screamed.

Mindy was a full-fledged werewolf now and all consumed by her new nature. Austin and Jamal were holding her back away from Alexa.

"Where is Tristan?" She pushed Jake in the chest as hard as she could, but he didn't budge at all.

Arthur's head was in his palms as he sat in the muddied snow.

"TELL ME!" Alexa dropped to the ground and hit him with all her might.

"He's gone…" Arthur cried.

"Gone where?" She begged as she pulled at his wrists.
"He's dead, Lex," Jake answered.

She collapsed to the ground and held her knees tight to her chest as she howled in pain.

"Lex," Jake hugged her gently.

The sobs were ear-splitting, a lot of the wolves who had control ran off to the river and bunker to escape the sorrow, and others were chaining the girls together trying to restrain them from hurting Alexa. Lucy and Elle were still safe as they could be inside the well, even if they were cold.

Lupe walked off behind the homes, this was too much for her. She was sickened by what she had walked into.
"What happened?" Alexa came up for air.

"The moon phase affected everyone ever affected by a werewolf, even the dead ones came back. His brothers were waiting for him," Jake explained.

"Jake!" I called him over.

"Some things don't need to be shared," I whispered as I hinted at *how* he died.

He nodded and agreed.

Flames lit up the back of the homes and embers and ash blew in our direction.

"FIRE!" Jax yelled as Graham and Clarence raced to diffuse them.

Lupe emerged with bottles of oil and matches as she continued to light up the remaining homes. There was enough natural gas running through this little town that it couldn't be stopped now.

"You crazy bitch!" Graham gripped her by the throat and slammed her into the ground.

"Let her up," Jax ordered.
Graham hesitated but obeyed Jax's demands.

"Why?" Jax growled at Lupe.

"You've learned nothing! Did I teach you anything?" she yelled in his face as her hands morphed with rage.

"Calm down Lupe," Joel begged.

"Stay out of this, Joel. I don't want to hurt you!" Lupe urged as her fangs tore through her gums.

"I wanted to do better…" Jax sighed.

"You've done worse! Look at these people around you, you did this! And you!" She pointed at me.

"I'm not innocent, I've killed! But I won't pretend I can be better," She flexed her hands at her side.

"We can try!" Jax argued.

"We shouldn't even be alive! We are an abomination to this planet, and we will spread like a disease until there is nothing left. What you have here is the minority who can control themselves. A minority, Jax! It's not enough…" she wept.

"She's right, it can't be contained," I agreed.

The flames grew bigger and hotter as we argued amongst ourselves. Most were against Lupe, some too nervous to agree and others still trying to find a way to make a meal of the three humans that remained here.
"It's a new world now pretty girl," Graham smiled with enthusiasm in his eyes.

"And you think it'll be any different, Graham? Do you think it'll be easier to hunt when there's nothing left? Do you think there'll be less politics or rules? There'll be more struggles now, more uncertainties, you won't last a month in a world of werewolves," she smiled.

Graham moved swiftly and, in a flash, he was a beast. He hovered over Lupe's body; he had taken her head clean off her body. It took a few seconds to realize what he had done and Jax and Joel had turned, I didn't realize it, but so had I, my muzzle was deep in his chest.

Chapter Fourteen

Jake

Blood drenched the snow and mud as the flames grew closer, the smell of hair singeing burnt my nostrils as the one pack had now divided into two. Graham's loyals were fighting against Jax's. I threw Alexa back into the well and covered the opening with my body as Mindy, Carrie, and the others thrashed about trying desperately to break the chains.

Carrie broke through first and beelined for Clarence, Celinde was right behind her as she ran to Christian's aid as he fought against Evan.

"Jake, get out of here!" Alexa pleaded.

"I'm not leaving you in there to die," I whispered into the well.

"Tell us what's happening!" Lucy begged.

"Jax is okay, he's fighting back-to-back with Joel and Noah," I explained.

"Graham's down," I added.

"Good!" Lucy clapped.

"Evan?" Alexa cringed.

"Your parents are tearing his limbs off as we speak," I gagged.

"That's comforting," she sighed.

"Why did he leave me, Jake?" Alexa asked.

"What do you mean?" I asked.

"I know he can handle himself and I know you all too well to believe he was killed. So, what happened?" She pressed.

"You should hear it from your father," I refused.

"Well, my father is off killing more werewolves again and you could get body slammed into this pit at any moment... You owe me, Jake!" She argued.

"He couldn't live with the grief a second time round, he loved you so much, he wanted you to know that," I cried.

"And then?" She wept as Elle and Lucy huddled together and held her upright in her grief.

"He threw himself into the triple tank of colloidal," I sighed.

There was no sound from the well at that moment, and then there was, Alexa, beating her hands raw into the bricks.

"Lex, STOP!" Elle begged.

"I can't stop, I can't live like this anymore!" She cried.

"What do we do?" Lucy asked me.

"We let her feel it," I reached into the well to help pull her out as Lucy pushed her up on her shoulders.

I handed her the hunting knife that Tristan had used to skin animals.

"The cars are that way, get out of here while they are distracted," I said as I pulled the other girls out.

Alexa hugged me tightly as she wept. Kitty hung back to stay with me, I was reluctant to let her, but she was slowing down Elle and Lucy with her foolishness.

"You've always been like a big, big brother to me, thank you," Alexa held me tighter.

"I love you too little one, be safe!" I smiled as she ran after Elle.

Cory was backing away from the fire when he erupted into a cloud of dust. Lupe's body was nothing but a black mark in the snow and Noah began to weaken and Jax was trying to hold him up.

The fighting was over, Graham's followers were dead or running north and our home was a pile of ash.

"What now?" I asked as I knelt beside Jax and Noah.

"I have a feeling I won't be around much longer," Noah coughed.

"No," Christian raced to his side. He had a broken arm and a deep laceration across his face. A lot of the others pulled up far worse.

"Hey, bud!" Noah held his shoulder.

"I'm sorry about Lupe," Christian wept.

"It's what she wanted, she wasn't herself, not like this," Tears streamed down Noah's face.

"In another life then," Christian held his hand.

"I already got a second chance, I blew it," he chuckled lightly.

"Third time lucky maybe," Christian snorted.

"Too much grief for one-lifetime brother," Noah sighed.

"Grief is the final act of love, right?" Christian nodded.

"So, they say," Noah agreed.

"I'll continue to miss you, my friend," Tears poured from Christian's eyes and Jax sat tight up against Noah.

"It was a pleasure to know you," Jax nudged him.

"And you, for all you've done and will continue to do..." Noah began to fade.

A moment passed and Noah was gone as the others congregated around us.

We huddled together as we knew a new world waited for us out there. Lupe's words were true, this was bigger than us now...

Chapter Fifteen

Carrie

We gathered anything salvageable from the remains of the fire and headed up toward the cars.

Some chose to stay behind; everyone was free to make their own choices now. Kamloops was empty so Kitty and Jake chose to start fresh and separate from the group, Arthur and Mindy did the same, they figured if Alexa ever came back, she'd know to look for them there.

Henry and Izzy went their own way with Serg; Fred and Jenson had perished in the fighting, so they agreed to keep Serg company along the way. They planned to cross Alaska into Russia and make their way down to Austria.

None of us knew what we were looking for anymore, we didn't know what was out there now, all we knew was a lot had happened and anything we came across would demand vigilance.

There weren't many of us left now; me, Jax, Ezra, Christian, Austin, Liam, and Celinde. Otis and Jamal stayed in the ash that was once Wolftown, they wanted to hunt through Yukon and were excited to have the opportunity, they had always been the live of the land kind of guys.

"Only seven of us left?" Ezra smiled as he leaned against the hood of the car.

"Guess I'll have to watch your back," I smiled.

"Celinde…" He started.

"I think she's okay, things are different now," I smiled.

"Her silence is the last warning she gives," He added.

"So always make her laugh!" I giggled.

"And us?" He asked softly.

"Friends, you'll always have a piece of me, Ezra," I smiled.

"Ouch," he laughed involuntarily.

"What good is it? There's no future for us in anything," I explained.

"There never was, but I kept you safe and sane and you lead me in times when my world was too dark…" he sighed.

"Look I can't give you a wedding, kids, I can't even give you a home, but I can promise I'll be here when you're not feeling your strongest, you don't have to carry everyone all the time, we can do that together," he brushed his thumb against my cheek, I was weak to his touch.

"Carry…good joke!" I chuckled.

"All organic! That's all I had," he smiled.

"Okay friends with benefits, but I have one condition," I added.

"Anything," he held me close.

"You dig all the toilet holes," I laughed.

"And mine!" Celinde added.

"I'll dig all of them if it keeps everyone sane," Ezra laughed.

"Good, you're going to need this!" Liam pressed a shovel into his hand.

"Who's riding with us?" I shouted.

"I will," Jax replied.

The others climbed into the last free car, and we drove south for more days than I wished to count.

America was quiet now, people were in hiding, and for good reason. What activity we did see was violence and survivors scurrying for shelter and searching desperately for supplies to ensure an unlikely survival.

People were fighting one another, killing even. And wolves were never far behind, the younger ones lurked about and let the humans kill each other off, it was an easy meal for them. It satiated the desire for murder for a short time.

My beast never returned, once the blood moon was gone, I felt a release. I wasn't carnal anymore, but my body was sore like I'd aged ten years in a matter of weeks. My hands were achy with an onset of arthritis, likely caused by the breaks I endured. Celinde felt the same, she would struggle in pain at night, and the cold brought on the worst of it.

We met a lot of our wolves along the way, everyone told us to stay north, as far north as we could, but Jax and Christian hadn't lost their do-gooder natures, Jax wanted to get us as far south as we could, he knew the warmer weather would help our conditions and there were human colonies surviving and re-building after the initial attacks, places we might be safe. We let him speculate all he wanted until the petrol stations began to dry up, and everything was at a standstill. Some cities were just operational, but there weren't many and for how long?

The odd werewolf who would engage with us was edgy and distressed. They were on the brink of overfeeding and had lost most of their senses. Ezra was the talker, and even he had trouble getting much out of them except that the entire west coast had been overrun, the mid-west wasn't far behind, but the south had enough warning to fight back and the south had a large population of armed citizens.

What we were told was that survivors had made a safe zone in Montgomery Alabama.

We took a short break on the side of the road to gather our thoughts and stretch our legs while Austin scoured an empty gas station for crumbs of food. He didn't need supersonic hearing to know our bellies were hungry.

"We need supplies," Christian announced as he took a turn towards Nashville.

"Shouldn't we keep a low profile?" I asked.

"There's a difference between them and us," he smiled.

"And what is that?" Celinde asked.

"We can control it, most of the time," he added.

"That's risky if they catch you," she began.

"If they catch us, they don't have a very good chance of killing us," he snickered.

"That's not helping my nerves," Celinde pinched his side.

"The others aren't going to like this, you're going into dangerous territory," she scowled.

"Isn't that the best way to go undetected, they won't expect it, especially with you two with us," he pleaded to seek her approval.

"It's the unassuming, Celinde. We'll load up with supplies and be gone in a day or two," Ezra pressed as he supported Christian.

"I don't agree with this…" I grumbled.

"You don't have to," Ezra flicked my hair back gently.

I was livid with Ezra; he had always consulted with me about decisions at the Precinct and suddenly we were rouge and my opinion meant nothing.

Ezra was smart, I knew and trusted he'd never do anything to land us in hot water, but now he was fighting for my survival. He didn't care if he was in harm's way, he knew Celinde and I couldn't keep living on salami sticks, twinkies, and gum. It was hard enough to come by any of that as it was. Gas stations were running on fumes, and we had barely enough to get us to Alabama.

The guys pushed the cars over ten miles to the nearest gas station while Celinde and I each steered. Liam was the first to wolf out to power himself through it. Austin wasn't far behind him, Ezra and Jax were the only ones who didn't change forms. Jax changing always scared me, he didn't know that, but I never knew if he'd come back, and without Lupe, Joel, or Lucy to trigger him we'd be lucky if we didn't lose him completely. His struggle was so well hidden, and I knew he found comfort in Noah, he found someone who could relate to his struggles, and in a second, he was gone. He wasn't the friend he wanted; he was the friend he needed.

"Ok, pull up here!" Jax panted.

"Where is here?" Ezra sighed.

"Columbiana," Celinde pointed at a sign.

"There's a lot of activity around here," Jax warned as we heard gunfire and tires screeching.

"Get out!" Ezra ordered as he yanked me from the car.

"Into the woods," He whispered.

Austin, Christian, and Liam were ahead of us as Jax helped Celinde over broken logs and ducked her behind a large tree as a flood of lights illuminated the forest. Night had come quickly, and hooligans were out hunting, we just didn't know what. We had to abandon the cars; we were on foot from here.

We hiked our way through the woods for hours more until we reach an abandoned mansion, it was an old wedding venue that boasted an eerily peaceful view of the Coosa River.

"Now what?" I asked Jax as we all sat on the stairs inside the large house.

It was far from elegance, this had been the scene of a massacre, the walls were strewn in blood splatter, and food was spilled over the floors and beginning to grow mold, but there were no bodies, they had taken those or maybe they were what had chased us here. There was a story that may never be told and all I could do was speculate as I gazed upon a beautiful wedding cake, rustic with now dried flowers, the only piece of the room that went untainted.

"We should see if there's any food in the kitchen, they have a generator," Celinde smiled as she held my hand.

Her grip wasn't strong anymore, she was weak and tired from the continuous travel and lack of sustenance.

I held her hand a little tighter as we looked around for a kitchen.

It was towards the back of the building and had double doors which lead into a large commercial kitchen.

Bingo! There was a huge fridge and an even bigger freezer.

"Jackpot! They are still running," Celinde gleamed as she opened the fridge.

"This stuff is still good," she declared.

"Not surprised, this place mustn't have been hit too long ago," I said with worry.

A week maybe two if the mold on the canapes was anything to go from. It was hairy and just sprouting, the humidity a major player in that advancement.

"There's steak, it smells okay. I'm willing to risk it," Celinde's eyes watered as she held it close to her face.

"Well, you better hope the plumbing is working, just encase," I said as I gazed upon the thick cut of ribeye.

"C'mon Carrie, STEAK! How long since you had a steak, I mean a good steak?" she pressed.

"I couldn't tell you," I smiled as I reached for the second steak she had pulled out.

"What is going on in here?" Liam asked as he moved through the saloon doors.

"We found steak!" Celinde gleamed.

Liam's eyes beamed with excitement as he walked towards the fridge and pulled out a rack of short ribs that had been marinating in vacuum-sealed bags.

"This is still good! Let's cook it up," he drooled.

Celinde was already firing up an oven and lighting a stove as Jax walked in with the others. Liam was throwing together something that resembled a salad with the vegetables that were still good in between eating sliced ham and cheese.

"I don't care how old it is, it's so good," he moaned with joy.

"Any bologna?" Ezra asked.

"You're a real classy guy, Ez" Jax laughed.

"I'm nostalgic," he retorted.

"Ohhh, mock it all you want but I'd kill for a bologna, cheese, and crisp grill right now," Austin agreed.

"Let's see what there is," I smiled as I turned on a light to a pantry in search of crisps while Ezra hunted through the fridge for bologna.

Celinde was heating a pan for our steaks and had the ribs in the oven while Liam diced potatoes and other hardier vegetables that managed to last.

"Has anyone checked for ice cream?" Austin asked.

"It's a wedding venue, I bet they have the best ice creams!" Celinde said excitedly.

Jax opened the freezer and revealed shelves full of cookie dough, ice cream, pies, more meat and vegetables, and dairy goods.

"I'm never leaving this place," Ezra smiled as he fell to his knees.

"We'll be leaving soon, that generator is going to run out of fuel and there's none here," Austin sighed.

"We'll take as much as we can," Jax nodded.

"I'll go find some bags," I said.

"I'll come with you," Austin nodded.

The other half of the venue was all lodgings, rooms were full of people's belongings, half-empty wine glasses, elegant gowns, and expensive suits and every room boasted a spa bath and beds softer than a cloud.

"I'm never going to be ready to leave this place," I sighed as I dropped the gown I held to my body and squeezed a fluffy pillow into the side of my face.

"I don't even remember what sleeping in a real bed is like," Austin collapsed into the perfectly made bad.

"Tonight's your night!" I grabbed his hand and pulled him up to help me look for bags.

"Take the suitcases and duffle bags," he suggested.

"Whoever survived took these people's cars," I grumbled.

"We can't take too much if we're on foot," I sighed as I pulled out woman's clothes from a duffle bag.

"We'll figure it out, Carrie," Austin smiled.

"Ya know, maybe when we get to this place, if it's all good. Maybe you and Celinde want to stay there?" he asked.

"Nope, I'm never leaving you guys. You're all my family now," I growled.

"Why would you say that?" I questioned.

"I see you struggling, I know it's getting harder to keep up with us," he replied.

"Sorry, am I slowing you down?" I said sarcastically.

"I don't mean like that, I just mean you might find some peace in a new place," he sighed with regret.

"A new place that I know nothing about with people who are edgy and unaware of what's out here, I know what it is though, and I've survived for a long time," I snapped.

"You survived because we let you survive because we aren't the same as them, we choose not to kill people. Carrie don't for a second underestimate the fact that one of us could tear your throat out in half a second, you were strong because we let you be strong, because the other's needed a strong figure, because Jax couldn't hold himself together, Tristan kept the Precinct afloat, without his hunting you'd have all been our dinner a very long time ago, not by choice, by necessity," Austin stood over me tall and a little darker than normal.

"And you think we didn't have a plan in the event it all went hairy? We were equipped and ready the minute one of you barked in the wrong direction," I growled.

"I don't want to fight with you, Carrie. Let's get these bags back to the kitchen," Austin grabbed two bags and headed down the stairs.

"If it works, then I'll stay," I sighed behind him.

"I'm not trying to push you out," he whispered with regret.

"I just know you can't change again, it didn't stay with you," he added.

"And it's sucked the life out of me, I know you know that too," I sunk my head as I admitted defeat.

"It seems to give you girls a rougher time than us guys," he sighed.

"I don't know, without a beard Ezra isn't all that," I laughed.

"I can hear everything, Carrie," Ezra shouted from the kitchen.

"I know," I whispered as Ezra came out into the hall.

"Was it your idea?" I asked as I looked up at Ezra.

"It was mine," Christian said as he joined us.

"Unexpected," I sighed.

"Celinde is in constant pain, I don't think you guys ever got the chance to heal properly after you turned and then turned back again. The first time I felt the pain for days, weeks even. But for you guys it hasn't gone away," he explained.

"It seems like you're getting worse," Jax said as he came through the doors with a bowl of ice cream.

"If it all checks out, just stay a while until we can find some help," Ezra pressed.

"Help? Who do you have in mind?" I laughed.

"Graham and Clarence mentioned witches, maybe..." Ezra began.

"If what they said about witches is true, they won't want to help us, they are probably plotting a way to at least condense this whole shit show," I sighed.

"Maybe so, but we have to try," Jax encouraged.

"Steaks are ready!" Celinde shouted.

"Don't say anything to her! Let her have one night," I ordered and they all nodded to agree.

V.J.Garland

CHAPTER SIXTEEN

JAX

Carrie sat on the cold steel countertop and ate a steak with her bare hands, Celinde was on the floor, hands deep in potatoes and ribs. They never showed how much they suffered for us. It had become such a pattern for them to be strong and hide concern from us. It was odd, we were the stronger species and yet here they were mothering us, going without, for us. All to protect us from becoming the worst versions of ourselves.

They were the best people I've ever known, and the worst. Carrie should have put me down a long time ago. Kyle should have, we might not be in this mess if he had. Noah's outbreak had traveled slowly, but we ensured its survival. Lupe did the right thing lighting up the Precinct, I just wish the rest of us perished with the others. It was an awful thought but when I think about what it had done to the lives of the people close to me, I felt sick.

Lucy and Alexa were out there alone, and I had no way of finding them, they were likely dead. Any car they had would draw attention and finding fuel for it would be even harder. Food wouldn't be too hard; Alexa was a skilled hunter and did a good job of living off the land when she was challenged to it.

Lucy was far less hardy, she valued cleanliness, home-cooked meals, a warm bed, and a good book. She would be okay with Alexa, but she'd be overwhelmed quickly.

I pitied Alexa, her heart was shattered over Tristan, what an awful life we lived to have our souls find their other half and have them quickly torn away so violently. Maybe we didn't deserve love, I sat in a room of beasts skilled in the art of murder.

"Jax," Celinde tossed me a slab of ribs.

"Thanks," I gleamed as I caught them.

Ezra was edgy, he knew there was something unusual about the way Carrie and Celinde were deteriorating.

We didn't have to speak; we did that with our eyes after so many years, Christian joined in as he turned his back to the girls while they were distracted shoveling mouthfuls of food down.

Carrie was the first one to pass out, she'd eaten and drank like a queen and would sleep just as well tonight, Ezra collected her in his arms and walked her to a bedroom. Christian was not far behind with Celinde propped up in his arms, she was still awake, but her senses dulled by the amount of wine she had drank.

"This room," I ushered them in and dimmed the lights. Carrie lay on one side of the king-size bed and Celinde on the other.

"Sleep well," Christian pecked Celinde on the forehead.

"You too," she smiled as she pulled the covers over her arms and tucked them into her neck.

"I'm going to take a real shower," Ezra exclaimed.

"About time," Liam chuckled.

"That's not kind," Ezra joked.

"I think I'm just used to his smell," Austin howled as we descended the stairs to the smaller rooms.

"Go shower, meet for beers on the deck in thirty minutes," Christian ordered.

"Deal!" I beamed.

I found an empty room with as little mess and blood splatter as possible and undressed in the bathroom, the room filled with steam. My first proper hot shower in years with decent pressure. The cold was so deeply embedded in me after so many years it should hurt, the water was so hot it scalded me, those scalds healed quickly just in time for new ones until I succumbed to defeat and turned the heat down.

The water around my feet was brown, a mixture of old blood, dirt, and skin. One of the grossest parts of being a werewolf was the constant shedding, not fur, skin. It was flaky and itchy and something I never got used to.

I grew tired of the consistent beard of necessity to blend in, but without it, I resembled more of a hormonal teenager, the raggedy skin from turning was insufferable for someone as old as I was. I didn't even know how old I was anymore, I was pushing 40, give or take. The years blended over time. Graham said they would, Clarence backed that. I was in for decades or centuries of the unknown— if I lasted that long.

My shower came to an end once the water ran clear and I felt a squeak when I rubbed my hair, a trick my mother had taught me when she got halfway through hairdressing school before she married well and lived life as a lady of luxury—meaning she went for tea and french pastries most days.

I trimmed my beard of its shaggy uneven ends and searched the bags in the room for men's clothing. There was an overnight bag with the bare minimum. Trackpants, a black singlet, and a navy zip-up jacket.

There were a cheap pair of slippers wrapped in plastic with wedding bells embroidered on them, so I slipped them on and headed out to the deck. Christian was the first one there with a cooler full of beers he had found tucked in the corner of the kitchen.

The deck was large with chairs and tables and hung over the Coosa River, it was peaceful until Ezra, Liam, and Austin arrived. They had always been the rowdier of the group.

Austin cracked a beer first and passed them around.

"What's that?" Liam asked as he peered down the river.

There was a small flicker of light coming closer to us.

"A lantern?" Ezra whispered as he peered closer.

Suddenly there were more lanterns and they edged closer, there had to be about ten of them, it was a group of people on kayaks.

"Hey!" Ezra yelled.
"Stay back! We don't want any trouble!" One woman yelled.

"We don't want to hurt anyone," Christian said as they paddled away from the dock.

"Are you yourselves?" Another asked as they slowed.
"Yes," he lied.

"Back the way we came, two miles up, there's a few kayaks left, paddle to Montgomery. Ask for Kaya!" They drifted with the current down the river.

"Thanks!" Ezra shouted.

"Let's go get them!" Liam nodded eagerly.

Austin agreed and skulled his bear and raced off before the rest of us.

"Really…" Christian sighed.

"I'm not going either," I laughed.

"We got this," Ezra smiled as he dashed off into the darkness with ease.

"They won't be long, don't worry," I reassured Christian.

"How many do you think they can carry," Christian laughed.

"Liam's a klutz, three max!" I chuckled over my second beer.

"Jokes aside, I wanted to ask how you're doing?" I sighed.

"Ughh, it's been a constant internal battle if I'm being honest, couldn't have been easy seeing Lupe?" he asked.

"Lupe was fighting her own demons I think, I'm glad she didn't have to live a full life like this, she would have ended up like Tristan, she's not rough around the edges like that," I said.

"It was odd seeing her distanced from Noah, they clung to each other in such a different way, I bet that was heartbreaking for him," Christian sighed sadly.

"I think what she felt was resentment, a lot had transpired since they separated, she hated it for taking him from her and suddenly she was the very thing she despised," I explained.

"And then to see you like that...," he added.

"Yeah, I could feel her rage a mile away," I huffed.

"It wasn't you; she just didn't want this *for* you," He pressed his hand to my shoulder to support me.

"I know, I just hope in the next life she can forgive us both," a tear escaped my eye.

"If there is another life and the same souls are meant to meet every time, do you think I'll find her again?" Christian's eyes welled.

"I think it was a case of the right person at the wrong time, she will wait for you," I smiled.

"What about Lucy?" Christian asked as he brushed a tear away.

"Same, same! Right person, wrong lifetime," I sighed.

"Do you think she's, okay?" he asked.

"Gosh, I hope so," I lowered my head.

"Alexa is the best person she could be with, she's fiery but she's got a good heart," he said.

"She's got a broken heart…" I added.

Christian knew as well as I did, that Alexa was erratic, we had covered for her and Tristan more times than we could count.

Lucy was more mature, and I knew she'd keep her in line if Alexa kept them fed, Alexa had grown up with werewolves, so I had to hope she could handle herself.
Ezra could be heard panting from a few hundred feet away, he was wolfed out and carrying three kayaks on his back, Liam had two and Austin another two.

"You guys are going to need another shower," Christian teased.

"You will too once we've paddled all the way to Montgomery," Austin smiled as he changed back a little smoother than he had in the past.
The others placed the remaining kayaks down and Liam began hauling food from the kitchen and placing it in the

hatches with bags of drinks and other supplies, what didn't fit we strapped to the front and back of the kayaks.

It was dawn and Ezra was asleep on the grass nestled into Liam when Carrie and Celinde walked out with cups of coffee.

"Woah, you guys had a big night," Carrie yawned, and she gawked around at the masses of littered beer bottles and cans observed the kayaks loaded for a journey.

"Some people paddled by, and told us where to find these, we shouldn't stay here too long," I sighed.

"Oh, just one more night!" Celinde argued.

"Can't risk it Cel, go shower, dress warmly, and pack what you might need. We're in for a long paddle, there are rapids so try to find ponchos or something to keep you dry," I suggested.

"Okay," Celinde slumped into Carrie and sipped at her coffee with closed eyes.

Christian was asleep on a deck chair and Austin had snuck off to a bed inside the house somewhere.

The girls took over the rest of the packing while I caught a few hours of sleep.

CHAPTER SEVENTEEN

CELINDE

The kayaks were already packed with food and water by the time we got to them. Carrie went in to pack us some clothes and toiletries.

Jax had gone to sleep on the bunk bed across from Austin so once we were done packing, we made some sandwiches with loaves of frozen bread we had found in the freezer to give them all a little more time to sleep.

We'd be leaving late afternoon at this rate and the river would be cold and dark.

"Torches?" Carrie asked as I buttered bread.

"I saw mini ones in the guest drawers in the rooms," I nodded.

"That'll have to do," she agreed as she went looking for them.

The trip down to Montgomery was going to be long. A full day and then some with breaks, I knew I didn't have it in me to continuously paddle for a whole day, two of the kayaks were doubles. They had been roped to the spare singles.

I knew the guys had planned to double us up with one of them and haul the singles just to be safe or if we lost one on the rapids.

Beasts, killers, monsters, they were all of the above, but they were our monsters, and what complex and wonderful monsters they were.

"Celinde?" Christian whispered from the saloon doors.

"Yeah?" I called back.

"Hi," he spoke nervously like we were meeting again for the first time.

"Hungry?" I asked as I offered him an egg salad sandwich.

"Sure," he took a bite from the sandwich.

"What's eating you?" I asked.

"Just all the uncertainty, it's gloomy," he sighed.

"Haven't we lived with uncertainty before though?" I asked reassuringly.

"We have," he brushed the hair off my cheek.

"And somehow we survive," I smiled as I held his hand still.

"But we're never really living, we're only ever surviving. I feel robbed," he sighed.

"Robbed?" I asked.

"Robbed of the life we should have had together, right person, wrong time," he whimpered.

"Christian… You are the right person, and this is all the time I've got," I smiled.

"So, we good?" he laughed.

"We good," I laughed as he pressed his form against mine and kissed me passionately.

I'd forgotten what it felt like to be held the way *he* holds me; he touched all the right places to make my skin tingle and my heart flutter. The way his mustache tickled my forehead and his body wrapped completely around mine, his mold fit mine perfectly.

Life at the Precinct was always fixated on supplies, on routine, about where our next meal was coming from, who was going to crack under pressure, and who the newest newcomer would be. It was a prison and I understood now why Lupina burnt it to the ground. We had lived a hyped-up version of her life with Noah. Jax had made a mockery of all the things she shared with him, and he didn't recognize any of it until it was embers flying in the wind.

I sat atop the bench with Christian between my legs and I just held his face in my hands, and he held mine. It was magic, I could see the struggle written in the lines on his forehead, the worry in his crow's feet, the pain in his eyes. I'd left him alone for so long, we went into this together with good intent, but we failed each other, I wouldn't do that again, and I wouldn't become dark Celinde.

I nested my head into the nook of his shoulder and neck and felt Carrie's eyes on me and Jax peered over the top of her head.

"Your turn," Jax chuckled as he nudged Carrie.

"That's different," she punched him in the arm.

"Why?" I asked loudly exposing their position.

They entered the kitchen and Christian reluctantly detached from me.

"Because I'm not like you," she stroked my arm.

"And that's okay," Christian smiled at her softly.

"I love Ezra, but that time has passed, and we are both better people when we aren't fixated on each other," she explained.

"I think we both knew it wasn't going to be forever," Ezra said as he pressed through the doors.

"We're werewolves, we don't get forever," Ezra sighed.

"Let's focus on the mission at hand," Carrie became more serious.

The mood in the room shifted as everyone began to busy themselves with preparation.

Everyone met in the blood-splattered hall one last time, before saying goodbye to fluffy beds and warm showers. We trickled out the door to the kayaks reluctantly, even if it did wreak of mold in this place.

Carrie and I jumped in a double together and the guys towed the spares behind two of them.

We paddled slowly, keeping pace with each other as we carefully observed our surroundings.

As the hours passed we saw the odd abandoned canoe or, kayak or paddle board. Signs of struggle and one with claw marks and blood all over it.

Passing through Wetumpka was tricky, it was clearly active with bad company, and the bridge over the river was broken as we paddled past the busier part of the town. Still populated with humans but the sound of werewolves lingered in the distance, the thrashing of cars being belted across the pavement. It was terrifying and we kept as close as we could to the others.

"Paddle faster," Jax ordered as he hooked his kayak to ours and began to haul us faster down the river.

"Slow down!" Carrie growled lowly.

"Hold on and tighten your life vest," Liam hissed, even though he was scared now.

They knew what we knew, if one of those werewolves wanted to eat us, there'd be nothing they could do about it, they could fight, but against so many, they'd lose.

"I'm scared, Care," I shook in fear as I rested my paddle on my legs.

"Me too," she sighed as she picked up her paddle and allowed the guys to tug us at speeds we couldn't keep up with.

The cramping was getting harder to avoid, moving from one position to another only delayed the discomfort for a short amount of time. We were moving at record speed now that we had passed all the rapids. We lost a few bags of supplies through those rough areas where things weren't tied down too well.

The next stretch was easy, or so it should be. We landed on a quiet bank for the night and made camp. Liam handed out sandwiches and beers and we all turned in extra early so we could be up at dawn. We should arrive in Montgomery sometime tomorrow and my fears were many.

None of us knew what to expect, weeks ago it could very well have been a safe place, but I knew that could change in an instant.

My eyes were heavy, my arms ached, and I felt the loom of sunstroke, the heat emitting off my forehead and cheeks even though spring was only just arriving.

Carrie was out cold next to me and grumbled in her sleep and I took the chance to cozy up with Christian while the others whispered between themselves.

There was such an emptiness without the others, and it was felt so clearly as if a part of the conversation was missing—nothing made sense.

We had left half our family behind, half of who we were. I hadn't really felt that loss yet, I hadn't felt anything in so long, I was tired of being afraid, tired of my fear stealing all the best moments away from me.

Christian pulled me closer as he felt all my self-doubt pile on top of me. He had this way of knowing when I was vulnerable. When he could, he wrapped me in his protective bubble and fought away all the bad parts of me.

He didn't have to do anything at all, his warmth was a gentle reminder I wasn't alone, and he'd never let me be alone.

"You're sore," he sighed as he rubbed my arms.

"It was a long day for us weak humans," I smiled up at him.

"Jump on with me tomorrow, you can navigate, I'll paddle" he pulled my hair back off my shoulders.

"Navigate?" I questioned.

"It's a messy water system, lots of off streams, we need to stay on course but in the lesser populated areas for as long as possible," he explained as Jax handed us a faded map they had found at the mansion.

"Through here," I suggested as I pointed to a stream named Gun Island Chute, it wrapped around the bottom end and would bring us out onto the Alabama river.

"That'll work," Jax agreed.

"You know we are in for miles of exposed waterways along here," I pointed to the weaving water trail we'd be paddling at dawn.

"This is the safest way," Liam nodded.

"I agree, but it's a flawed plan," I sighed as I place the map down.

"Flawed is all we've got right now," Ezra winced.

"Get some sleep everyone, we're in for a long day tomorrow," Austin yawned.

"I'm going to keep watch," Jax announced.

"I'll take the second shift," Christian nodded as he offered me his arm as a pillow.

CHAPTER EIGHTEEN

LIAM

The next day drowned us in sunlight too early, Jax was asleep against a tree. Carrie was up sipping on cold instant coffee, she must have taken over the watch. Christian showed no signs of having moved from Celinde's side and she had his arm firmly locked under her chin.

Ezra was next to wake, he was straight to Carrie's side to steal her coffee, one sip and he was bounding about waking everyone else and tossing everyone bags of sugary cereal.

"Gross," Celinde exclaimed as she tossed the cereal back at him.

"It's the only cereal they had there," he laughed as he tossed it back at her.

"I'll starve," she muttered as she curled back into Christian.

"Come on guys, eat something, we've got a long trek ahead," Carrie ordered softly.

"Yes, Mom," Austin yawned.

Austin pulled out a bag of powdered milk and some dried oats. We'd lost a lot of our food supplies coming through the rapids.

Everyone huddled around to eat some food, most of us opting for dry cereal and eating it like chips. Jax and Christian were getting the kayaks ready. Celinde climbed into a double with Christian and Carrie into a double with Ezra. The rest of us took the singles and we left the two spares behind. We were on the final leg of the journey, or so we hoped.

The constant paddling was more tiring the second day in a row. It was challenging to avoid humans and werewolves, nobody traveled together the way we were, and we were vastly different. We were natural enemies of one another and that wouldn't be easy to explain to either species.

"How far now?" Carrie sighed.

"One more bend, there's a lot more activity around here," Celinde kept her voice low.

Carrie held her gun a little closer now, it wasn't unlike her to be armed. Life at the Precinct taught her she had to be prepared even if it bought her only seconds.

Celinde was more hesitant to carry firearms. Christian always made sure she had something, pepper spray, or a knife, the basics but she hated the idea, she was the more tender soul of the girls.

As we floated passively into the cityscape of Montgomery fires were blazing inland coming from suburban areas. A large cage had been erected around a portion of the city, the I65 was a warning sign for any werewolf, it was dressed in the heads of hundreds of wolves as if they were fourth of July decorations. We pulled to the side before we got underneath it and made our way into the city. It was heavily manned by an army of militia.

"We need help," Carrie begged as she was dragged to the ground by a fiery guard who approached us as soon as we had disembarked.

Jax was uneasy and his eyes began to beam notes of yellow, Ezra held his arm, urging him to trust Carrie's process.

Jax's eyes had never been yellow in all the years I had known him. I didn't even know they could change back once you had gone over the edge. I knew if Ezra let him go right now they wouldn't be yellow for much longer.

The guard pressed Carrie's chest with a shotgun teasingly as he looked at the rest of us and she screamed and begged for mercy.

"What do you want?" Another guard approached and looked Celinde up and down.

"Maybe this was a bad idea," Austin scowled as he began to feel uneasy in his skin.

"We heard this was a safe place for humans," Celinde yelled as she cried for Carrie under the weight of the gun.

"How do I know you're human?" he asked.

"Why would we risk coming to a human colony if we weren't?" Celinde shouted.

Five other guards came through the barbed wire fencing, it wasn't any sub-par fencing it was thick, barbed at every angle, the tops had revolving blades constantly spinning and in case that didn't ward you off, they had live werewolves captured and imprisoned inside thick cages as a warning to every other werewolf. They were mostly small werewolves, cages like that wouldn't contain fully grown men, definitely not wolves of Ezra or Jax's size.

"We'll see," Another guard nodded to another, and they approached with three dogs. Two Dobermans and one Rottweiler.

The dogs snarled over Carrie and sniffed at her with slight confusion. They weren't sure of her, inevitably they backed away and the guards let her stand as the dogs moved to Celinde.

Celinde was frozen, she let the dogs sniff her hand, they seemed to spend more time on her, Christian's scent on her was a clear trigger as they barred their teeth somewhat but inevitably moved on.

Jax's face swelled as his fangs became ready to defend his family, but he kept it hidden as best he could. Ezra was approached next by the dogs and guards.

They were on edge around him and began to snarl and bark. The guards raised their guns and kicked Ezra to the ground.

"You're one of them!" A guard yelled.

"No!" Celinde cried in defense.

"What about the rest of you," another guard pointed his gun at Austin while the others zoned in on the rest of us.

"We're different," Christian argued.

"Different?" a guard laughed.

"We can control it," Christian shouted as he admitted our truth.

"Let's see about that," the first guard grabbed Carrie by the hair and threw her down facing the rest of us, she was suspended on her hands and knees with the guard pressing the gun into her body.

"Can you control it now?" He cocked his gun, pointed it at Carrie's head, and fired a shot. Her body hit the ground hard, and blood splattered everyone in a three-meter radius.

Ezra's fangs were deep in the killer's neck before any of us could blink, Jax was tearing through the dogs, Celinde raced to Carrie's body and held her as she wailed in the torture of losing her best friend, her only human companion.

Celinde's pain was enough to send Christian into a rage, he tore his claws through the fence while guns rained bullets down on him. He pushed through and tore the first cage open unleashing a starved teenager. He leaped through the second line of fencing and ripped the guards from their towers.

Christian collapsed to the ground, his body riddled with bullets unable to keep up with itself.

"No Christian!" Celinde raced to his aid, I was steps behind her as he fought to relieve his body of the pellets.

Celinde's hands were deep in the crevices trying to pull out every piece of lead she could find.

His body began to turn slowly exposing the real damage. He was mortally wounded. Something we never thought could happen.

Jax raced to Christian's side doing what he could to stop the bleeding.

"JAX! Help him," Celinde screamed.

"I can't," he cried.

"Yes, you can, you're a doctor! Save him!" She yelled.

"Celinde…" tears filled my eyes and obstructed my vision with blurs.

"He's gone, Celinde," Jax grabbed her and held her as she sobbed.

"He's not, he can come back!" She wept.

"He's lost too much blood, even werewolves need blood," Jax sighed.

Celinde raced to the closest body and used all her adrenaline to lug the body to Christian.

"Feed! Christian it's okay!" she pressed the bloodied body to his face.

But Christian didn't respond, he was gone.

She kicked the body away and collapsed onto him.

"You can't leave me, I can't lose both of you," she sobbed loudly.

Ezra was silent and in pieces as he picked up Carrie's body and lay it beside Christian's.

"Why did we come here!" Austin yelled as he kicked at the dead bodies.

Jax was turning again as he hovered over us all.

"What are you doing?" I asked.

He collected the bodies in one swift movement and Ezra picked up Celinde. The guards we had just killed were beginning to turn and we were vastly outnumbered.

"RUN!" Austin shouted.

V.J.Garland

V.J.Garland

V.J.Garland

V.J.Garland

V.J.Garland

V.J.Garland

V.J.Garland

Hunter's Moon: The Precinct

V.J.Garland